GW01048781

SWORDBEARER

A Family History novel

By

Robert Merry

Dedicated to my wife, Peggy

PREFACE

The "hero" of this book is Isaac Forster, a sail-maker from King's Lynn, who lived in the eighteenth century. He served his community in various capacities, ultimately becoming the Swordbearer of the town. Isaac Forster was my Great-great-great-great-great Grandfather on my father's side.

I first started tracing my family history over forty years ago. I had been inspired by a partial family tree given to me by my maternal grandmother, which traced a line back to the seventeenth century. I was later able to take this further and trace my lineage back for over thirty generations. This side of the family was quite straightforward, since I started out with so much information, but this book is not about this maternal line.

My father's side was more problematic. He knew that he had been adopted and his adoptive mother's surname was Merry, the name I now bear. When he was growing up, my father thought that he had a double-barrelled name, Merry-Forster, and, after joining the Army, decided to have this changed by deed poll, as he didn't think a double-barrelled name was suitable for a private in the Rifle Brigade. So he became simply Merry, usually known as "Tom", after a well known comic book character of the 1920s and 30s, even though his real forenames were Leonard Charles.

This was all I knew when I first tried to trace his birth certificate at St Catherine's House, where the registers were stored in the 1970s. At first I drew a blank; no Leonard Merry or Leonard Merry-Forster. Then I tried Leonard Forster and there he was. When I received the actual birth certificate, the mystery was solved; he had been given Merry as one of his forenames – Leonard Charles Merry Forster; so not double-barrelled after all. He had been adopted soon after birth and his new mother had included his new family name.

I could then start tracing the Forsters and managed to go back three generations to a ladies' shoemaker, Isaac Forster, who lived in various parts of London, mostly around the Soho and Covent Garden area. To go back further, I would need to find out where he was born and so I started to search the 1851 census. I was able to visit London occasionally as part of my work and spent many hours in an archive in Portugal Street, reading through reel after reel of microfilm for the centre of London, without success. This was long before the days of the internet and easy access to records.

In fact, it was nearly twenty years before I had a breakthrough. A local family history group had transcribed most of the 1851 census for London and I could buy a copy of this on microfiche. When I checked this, I soon found Isaac Forster and discovered the number of the microfilm reel I needed. On checking back to my original notes, I found that it was only two reels away from where I had finished before, when a change in my work had stopped my trips to London.

I continued my research at the local Family History Library of the Church of Latter Day Saints (LDS). I soon found out that this Isaac had been born in King's Lynn and, using copies of parish registers, obtained through the LDS, I was able to extend the line back another three generations. The earliest Forster I found was another Isaac Forster. One fact about him particularly struck a resonance with me; against the entry for his burial, there was the word "Swordbearer". As someone who had been interested in the sport of fencing since the age of sixteen and who was now a fencing coach, I needed to know more about this and devoted quite a bit of research time discovering more about Isaac, including visits to King's Lynn.

Eventually, I decided to write this novel based on Isaac's life and broadened my research to include people who had been part of his life; his master, his fellow workers, other townspeople, etc. I also had to read up about what life was like in the eighteenth century, both in King's Lynn and nationally. I have included at the end of this book a series of notes, which will enable the reader to separate fact from fiction. Most of the people mentioned in this book were real people and I have used their real names and, where I have been able to discover them, their occupations, but it is impossible to find out everything about them, so I have had to use my imagination quite a lot. Unlike many historical novels, this is not a tale of people who strutted the national and international stage and whose deeds are recorded in the history books. This is a simple story about ordinary people living ordinary lives in King's Lynn. I hope that it will still make an enjoyable and intriguing read. I hope it will encourage other people to look beyond a family tree as simply a list of names and dates, but also to find out more about the lives they led.

Robert Merry

Chapter One: A New Beginning

20th May 1736. It was already light by the time Isaac left his master's house in South Lynn, where he lodged. He had been woken as usual by the church bell being rung at four o'clock and would, as he had done for the past seven years, normally have set out for work to arrive at first light. But today was to be different. Although it was Thursday, not Sunday, Isaac wore his best clothes and a freshly powdered wig. He walked with a spring in his step in the bright sunshine, enjoying the early morning warmth. Although he was later than usual, he had his master's permission to take an extra hour on this special day.

He crossed the small bridge over the inlet, known as Ball (or Boal) Fleet, that led in from the river Ouse, and walked onto Boal Lane, alongside the river side. As usual, the quays along the water's edge were crowded with boats and there was a bustle of activity, stretching along the quays, as far as the eye could see. The vessels tied up at the water's edge were mostly small merchant packets, trading in a variety of goods from around the different coastal ports of England and even beyond, but Isaac also could see a larger collier a few hundred yards along the quays, near the Custom House. This type of boat, with its wider and shallower draught, was able to navigate the river to the port of Lynn, in spite of its size. He guessed that it had brought in coal from one of the Northern ports. Indeed, Isaac was quite right in his supposition, as the boat had arrived on the morning tide, with a load of coal from Newcastle. Isaac watched the busy scene, with goods being unloaded and loaded, moving to and from the nearby warehouses. King's Lynn was one of the busiest ports in England, serving as a gateway for most of Norfolk, Suffolk and beyond. The coal from the collier was bound for Norwich, to service its industries. The various taxes that Norwich paid would enrich the town of King's Lynn, who used much of it to support the poor of the town. A large proportion of the other tolls paid on goods being imported were paid to the Duchy of Cornwall, part of the heritage of the King's eldest son, the Prince of Wales.

Isaac turned away from the river into a courtyard, surrounded by a number of large buildings, their lower parts being built of brick, as a defence against flooding, whilst the upper levels were mostly clad in wood. He crossed the yard and entered a door at the far side. It was dark inside, but Isaac knew from experience where he was; the small warehouse that served as a storeroom. He was hit by the mixture of distinctive aromas; the mustiness of the bolts of linen canvas, the tar and hemp mixture from freshly made rope and twine. It had been part of his life for the past seven years.

He made his way across the floor to a door at the end of the room, which led him once more into the light. He was now in a large room, known as a sail loft. The floor was large enough to lay the pattern, using twine stretched between awls screwed into the wooden floor, for even the largest mainsail. There were several windows on the side nearest the courtyard, giving a good working light during much of the day. These were the business premises of his master, William Elstobb, master sail maker.

In the room, two young men were at work, seated at benches and sewing strips of canvas together, which would eventually become a sail. Two other benches stood unoccupied. Normally, Isaac would have been working at one alongside them, threading the triangular shaped needle, fashioned from a piece of whale-bone about four inches long, with linen thread, lubricated by beeswax, and forcing it through the canvas with the stitching palm, made from strong leather, or even metal, and attached to the palm of the right hand. As he came into the loft, the two men looked up from their work and smiled. These were the master's two sons. The eldest was William junior, who was eleven years older than Isaac and an experienced sail maker. The younger brother, Nicholas, was two years younger than Isaac and still to finish his apprenticeship. As they worked, they held the canvas taut between their left hand and a benchhook, otherwise known as a "third hand". This would keep the seams straight, whilst they sewed them with the right hand. Isaac waved a cheery greeting in their direction and continued on towards the small office in the far corner of the loft, where he knew he would find his master.

He knocked at the door and waited for the summons from the interior of the office before entering. Behind the desk sat William Elstobb. He stood up and extended his hand towards Isaac, who took it and shook it warmly. The firm grip and sprightly demeanour belied the master's sixty-five years. The hand now gripping Isaac's was hardened and calloused after many years of handling canvas. The features of his face, that were framed by his white hair and beard, also showed the effects of many hours spent in the open air in all weathers. His piercing blue eyes contrasted with his ruddy features and seemed to sparkle with the good humour that characterised the man.

Although principally a sail maker, William had other business interests and spent many hours out of the loft, mainly at the quayside, negotiating with various captains and ship owners to supply their sails. He also rented a section of the quayside nearby, which allowed him to charge ships moorage and collect the various tolls and taxes that were due. For his pains, he was allowed to keep a quarter of these tolls, before passing the rest on to the town chamberlain.

Releasing his grip, he motioned to Isaac to sit in the chair opposite the desk. To Isaac, William Elstobb was a father figure. Isaac's own parents had both died before his tenth birthday and he had been left in the care of the parish. He had been given some schooling, learning to read and write, and, at the age of fourteen, he had been apprenticed to William, who had been paid by the parish from charity funds given by rich benefactors for this purpose. His master had welcomed him into his own home and supplied his needs for food and clothing. He had then set about teaching him the skills of the sail maker's craft. Now, after seven years, Isaac had completed his apprenticeship and stood on the edge of full manhood.

"Well, lad," said the elder man, as he eased back into his own chair, "you've made it and I'm pleased with the result." Isaac smiled at the compliment, a rare offering from a man who could also be a hard task master at times. William Elstobb expected, and got, high standards and long hours of work in return for Isaac's training. "There's a job for you here in the loft for the time being. I'm willing to offer you thirty pounds a year, if that's acceptable."

"Thank you," replied Isaac, "I'll be honoured to work for you, sir."

"Then it's settled. If you wish to continue to stay with me and Margaret as our lodger, we'll discuss your rent later." At this William reached to a shelf behind him and picked up a jug and two mugs. "Only small beer at the moment, I'm afraid. Perhaps something stronger at the end of the day, but you'll need a clear head this morning."

Isaac took the proffered mug and drank the rather weak tasting beer. This was the usual drink in the loft and was much safer to drink than the water. Still, he thought, it was refreshing after his walk.

After the mugs were drained, William stood up and announced, "Now we have to make it all official. Time for a walk." The two men left the office and, leaving the brothers at their work, left by another door that led out into a narrow passageway, which they followed until they came to Lath Street,.

The two men turned left and walked up the street. Ahead they could see St Margaret's Church, with its two square towers flanking the main doors. The nearest tower was topped by a steeple that reached skywards. Along Lath Street were a number of large houses that were owned by some of the richest merchants in the town. They continued past the churchyard, the church itself and then crossed the site of the Saturday Market to the doors of the Guildhall, which they entered and climbed a flight of stairs.

This was the first time Isaac had ever been in this building. He knew it was where the governance of the town was carried out by the Mayor and Aldermen, but he had not had any business there before today. He now found himself in a lobby, where he joined his master and sat with him on a bench.

A door opened further down the passageway, which Isaac discovered much later in life to be the Robing Room. A number of gentlemen, resplendent in their scarlet and black robes of office, emerged and walked in procession down the corridor. William stood up, half dragging Isaac to his feet at the same time. They stood respectfully, heads slightly bowed, as the Mayor, Aldermen and Councillors of King's Lynn passed by and went through the doors of the main council chamber. Isaac and his master were able to sit back down on the bench.

After a few minutes, another man emerged from the council chamber. William spoke with him for a minute or two and then introduced him to Isaac as the Town Clerk. Isaac was handed a piece of parchment and urged to study it. On it were written the words of the oath he would soon take on becoming a freeman of King's Lynn. All those apprenticed to a freeman of the borough could, on completion of their apprenticeship, become freemen themselves and enjoy the privileges with which that status endowed them.

Once more the two men were left alone in the lobby, hearing nothing but the faint murmuring of debate beyond the door through where the Town Clerk had exited. William seemed to be almost half asleep, as he relaxed with the patience of one who had experienced this before, whilst Isaac read and re-read the parchment many times until he had almost memorised the words of the ancient oath.

After what seemed like an eternity, for this was to be the last business before the end of today's meeting, the door opened again and they were summoned into the main hall. This was a large room and Isaac saw the Mayor, Thomas Exton, and another twenty Aldermen and Common Councillors, sitting at the far end of the hall, in front of an impressive stained glass window.

Isaac's footsteps echoed as he crossed the stone floor to approach the assembled officials, with his master beside him. The Mayor started by asking William about his apprentice; whether he had satisfactorily completed his apprenticeship, was he of good character, and so on. William presented the Indenture with the terms of the apprenticeship to the Mayor, who spent a few minutes studying the parchment. Then he asked the assembled council for those willing to stand surety for Isaac's good behaviour and two of them raised their hands. Eventually, the Mayor turned to Isaac.

"Young man, are you ready to accept the freedom of this borough and all the burdens of responsibility that lays on you?"

"I am, your Worship." Isaac's voice cracked slightly and he wished again for that mug of small beer he had enjoyed earlier.

The Town Clerk moved forwards, bearing the Holy Bible and motioned to Isaac to rest his right hand on it.

"Now read the oath, lad," he said in almost a whisper.

Isaac lifted up the paper still clutched in his left hand and began to read the oath, scarcely changed over the centuries, that all those admitted as freemen of the borough of King's Lynn had taken.

"This hear ye Mr Mayor, that I, Isaac Forster, the franchise of this town of Lynn shall truly maintain to my power, as well without as within, and obedient be to you Mr. Mayor and to your successors, Mayors of Lynn; and to be aiding and assisting to the officers of the town in doing their office as need shall require, and the counsel of this town truly keep, and that I shall colour no bargain or sale contrary to the privilege thereof, and that I shall all other things do that belong to a burgess to do. So God me help."

Isaac struggled a little with the archaic language, but eventually reached the end. He was startled out of his state of concentration by the sound of applause. As he looked up, he saw that all the assembled dignitaries were clapping. The Mayor smiled at him and beckoned him forward. As he hesitated, his master gave him a gentle push in the back to help him forward.

As he approached, the Mayor rose from his chair and stretched out his hand. For the second time that morning, Isaac received a congratulatory handshake. Then the Mayor presented him with a parchment, decorated with a ribbon affixed by the seal of the town. This was his evidence of the Freedom of King's Lynn, with all its privileges and voting rights. As he turned away, he saw a broad smile on the face of William Elstobb.

A few minutes later, Isaac and his master were outside and walking back towards the sail loft. But now, Isaac felt different. He was twenty-one years of age, a time-served sail maker, a freeman of the borough and for the first time in his life he felt that he had truly entered the adult world. This was a new beginning.

Chapter Two: High Days and Holidays

Later that evening, Isaac was back in his room at his master's house. He lay on his bed and relived the events of the day; the ceremony at the Guildhall, the congratulations of those present, further good words from the Elstobb brothers and the celebratory drinks on the way home. This had been his coming of age and he felt excitement at the prospect of how his life would now progress. It wasn't only today that had brought new promise, for there had been other things happening in the last month that he felt could have a bearing on his future. These had started at Easter.

Easter Day was much later than usual in 1736. In fact, it was as late as it could be, on April 25th. The good news for Isaac and his two working companions had been that there were to be more days away from the sail loft than usual this year, since, as well as Good Friday and Easter Day itself, the following Tuesday had also been declared a holiday, in honour of the Royal marriage between Frederick, the Prince of Wales, and his seventeen year old bride, Princess Augusta of Saxe-Gotha-Altenburg, who married that day in London. The senior William Elstobb, whilst welcoming the holiday, was not so keen on missing another day's work, however, and grumbled a bit about it. With spring had come an upsurge in work at the shipbuilders, as they added to the fleet of around a hundred boats that called Lynn their home port. The winter storms had also wrought damage on many sails, so the Elstobb order book was full and there would be plenty to keep them occupied.

The Elstobb family were regular church-goers and Isaac, throughout his apprenticeship, had joined them. It was expected of him and it was also expected that he would take the sacrament several times a year, especially at the major holy festivals. England was a Protestant country and this observance showed loyalty to the established Church.

The Elstobbs had lived in South Lynn for most of their lives. South Lynn was separated from the main town centre by the Ball Fleet and had always been considered to be the poorer parish. There had been a certain amount of ill-feeling directed towards the King's Lynn corporation, who tried to foist their poor children and others dependent on parish aid onto South Lynn. South Lynn, however, did have one great asset. It was not as built upon as the main town and encompassed quite a lot of agricultural land. Once they had realised the value of this and obtained a fair rent from the corporation to support their parish, things had become much more equitable.

Although they would on occasions walk into King's Lynn centre to attend a service at Saint Margaret's church, or Saint Nicholas' Chapel, the Elstobb family and Isaac were more likely to go to the local South Lynn church of All Saints. The vicar here, the Reverend Doctor Thomas Pyle MA, had been there for as long as Isaac could remember, having come to the parish when Isaac was a small child. Thomas Pyle had also been made curate of St Margaret's and St Nicholas about five years previously, so he was kept quite busy on Sundays, sometimes taking three or more services around the town. He was renowned as a fiery preacher and strong advocate of the Protestant faith.

As this was to be the first service of the day, the Mayor and Aldermen had come to the parish, which meant that the Revd. Pyle had conducted the service himself. Isaac and the Elstobbs had occupied their usual position in a pew towards the rear of the small church. Proceedings had started when the church doors had opened and the Mayor's procession had been announced, causing everyone to stand. The procession had been led two men in ceremonial dress carrying long staffs. He was followed by four more men, also dressed in the uniform of their office, consisting of long black coats and bicorn hats, trimmed with gold braid. They carried the ceremonial maces of the town. Behind them was the Swordbearer, in similar ceremonial dress and carrying a large two-handed sword of mediaeval pattern, still in its sheath and with the point towards the roof. This was King John's Sword, which local legend had insisted was given to the town by King John himself, when he first gave a charter to the town, although the sword was, in fact, much later in date. Behind the Swordbearer came the Mayor, Aldermen and Councillors of the town.

The procession passed down the aisle until the Mayor and Aldermen took their places in the front pews, near the screen that separated the nave from the chancel. The Swordbearer took the sword and placed it in a purpose-built holder mounted on the wall to the left of the chancel arch, whilst the maces were placed in a stand placed nearby for that purpose. Then the vicar entered the church, walked down the aisle and took his place at the front. The service could begin.

It had been a warm day, the service was long and Isaac's attention had begun to wander. He looked around him to see who else was in the congregation. As he glanced across to the other side of the aisle, he noticed a family group that he did not recognise; a man, his wife, two boys of about ten or twelve, and a girl of around eighteen. It was the girl who had been the principal object of Isaac's attention. He had been struck by her pale features and the apparent softness of her face. He had noticed too the fair hair forming ringlets from beneath her bonnet. She appeared to be dressed well, although this was not unusual. Most people, whether rich or poor, dressed in a similar fashion; the main differences lay in the materials used for the clothes. Isaac's own jacket and breeches were of the same basic style as that of one of the richer merchants he saw around town. But whereas they might have clothes made of silk, his were mostly wool or worsted. However, it hadn't been her clothes that occupied his mind for the rest of the service.

As they left the church at the end of the service, Isaac had asked his master if he knew the family. William had responded with a laugh, "I wonder which one you're interested in, eh?" Isaac felt a bit hot and knew he was blushing. He had muttered something, but it made little sense. William laughed again, "They are the Bonner family. They're new to the parish. Thomas, the father, has just taken on the *Eight Bells* ale house. Perhaps you should pay it a visit sometime." At this William had walked away chuckling and started a conversation with his sons. They, in turn, looked round at Isaac, with broad grins on their faces. Isaac knew he was blushing again. He looked across towards the Bonners, only to find the girl looking at him. She briefly lowered the fan she was holding in front of her face and smiled at him. For a moment their eyes met, before Isaac looked away and went to join the rest.

During his apprenticeship, there were certain standards of behaviour that were expected of Isaac, under the terms of his indenture. He could not frequent certain places, such as ale houses, although there had been the occasional lapse in that respect, aided by William junior. Neither could he marry. During some of the various festivities that brought the community together, Isaac had met with some of the local girls, but, apart from exchanging friendly banter and joining in the dancing, had not been involved in any serious relationships. Isaac was quite a shy type in a lot of ways, but now he felt that it was time to explore more of his new freedoms.

*   *   *   *   *

On the Tuesday, the two Elstobb sons and Isaac had decided to go into town to join in the celebrations of the Royal wedding. This suited William and Margaret, as they could spend the rest day quietly together. At around nine o'clock, the three younger men left the house and walked across the bridge into the main town of King's Lynn. Their first destination was the church of Saint Margaret's, not to attend the service, but because they knew that this would be where the day's celebrations would start. There was already quite a crowd there when they arrived, mostly standing across from the main doors of the church. The three moved to join them. To the left was the Guildhall and across the road and between the Guildhall and the church was a space known as the Saturday Market Place. There was another building attached to the church, which was formerly the charnel house, but which now housed the town's grammar school. On a Saturday, the area would be crowded with stalls, but today this was empty, except for six cannon, that had been brought from Saint Ann's Fort, the fortifications north of the town that commanded a good view of the Wash and the approaches to the port. A number of militia were standing around, engaged for the most part in idle conversation. From the church could just be heard the sound of music from the service.

After some twenty minutes of waiting, the church doors were opened and the Mayor's procession came out. This was almost identical to the one at All Saints on Easter Day, except that there even more Aldermen and Councillors in attendance. The militia were now standing by their guns in a state of readiness, as the procession crossed over to the entrance to the Guildhall. The Mayor and corporation formed up in front of the Guildhall. An order was given and the cannon began to fire the salute. The noise was deafening in the confines of the buildings and acrid smoke from the blank shot and powder filled the air. At the conclusion of the salute, the Mayor attempted to make a speech, probably to wish the Royal couple well, but his words were mostly lost on the crowd, whose ears were still ringing and were conversing with all around about the experience they had just had. Eventually, the Mayor and his entourage moved away into the Guildhall for what everyone knew would be a day of feasting and supping good wine at the town's expense.

As the crowd started to disperse, Isaac and the brothers followed the route favoured by the majority; to the right of the Guildhall and along Briggate to the Tuesday Market Place. This was a much larger area than the Saturday Market Place, being a large square, and was the centre of much of the town's life and, sometimes, death. Here, each week, there was a market where all manner of people from the surrounding countryside could come and sell their produce. As one of the biggest markets in this part of the country, there would also be merchants there from as far away as London, or even from the Continent. It was said that you could buy all manner of goods there, from a bunch of blue ribbon right up to ready made panels to build a house.

As the trio entered the large square, they looked around at the throng of the townspeople that now filled the space inside the low wooden railings that surrounded the market square. To their left they could see the *Angel* ale house. To the right of the square was a large house, called the *Duke's Head*. The *Duke's Head* had originally been built for Sir John Turner, in 1683, and named in honour of the then Duke of York. Since then it had been the town house of the Turner family and was also, in part, a hostelry. Beyond the *Duke's Head* was a smaller hostelry, the *Mayde's*

Head. Between tese two hostelries were the pillory and whipping post, for the punishment of miscreants was often done publicly. There were even times when gallows had to be erected near to the market cross in the centre of the square.

The market cross was an imposing edifice, that had been designed and built under the supervision of Henry Bell about a quarter of a century earlier. It was basically a two storey building, octagonal in shape, topped by a wooden dome and a small tower topped by the cross itself. The first floor had a balcony, from where those charged with keeping order could look out over the heads of the populace. This was supported on sixteen Ionic columns. In the base of the building there was enough room to house a sort of guardroom for the use of the local "Red Coats", ostensibly there to protect the populace and keep order, but in reality a group of pensioners from the almshouses, who spent much of their time chatting and drinking ale fetched from the Duke's Head. On either side of the cross, as well as at its rear, there were curved arcades, with wooden roofs to protect against the weather, where traders could set up their stalls. Other semi-permanent stalls were made available around the periphery of the market place. Although Isaac and the brothers could not see it, since the larger buildings on the right of the square blocked the view, they were aware that, as they moved across the Tuesday Market Place, the skyline would be dominated by the spire of St Nicholas' Chapel, that lay to the north east of the square..

But the trio were not there for the sights, which were all too familiar to them. They were there to enjoy this special feast day. Whilst the councillors were in the Guildhall enjoying their feast, they had thought to provide food and drink for the populace. Spits had been set up near the centre of the square and various meats, from whole pigs to a side of beef, were even now filling the air with the delightful smell of cooking. There were stalls offering bread to accompany the meat, whilst the hostelries around the market place had also taken stalls from which to serve ale. The three adventurers had thoughtfully brought tankards with them in anticipation of this largesse.

In one corner of the square, there was a stage set up to present a number of performances to a large and rather noisy crowd. These spectacles ranged from complete short plays, including Dido and Aeneas (or The Prince of Troy), to performing animals. Other acts were more in a vein to please the main population, such as a girl of around twenty-five who balanced quart pots of ale on the hilt of a sword, whilst holding it in her mouth by the point. She also performed a whirling dance, spinning around rapidly for what seemed like several hundred times without stop. Another popular entertainment was the troupe of actors dressed as characters from the Italian Commedia dell'Arte; Harlequin, Columbine, Punchinello, Scaramouche and the rest. Their antics and buffoonery kept Isaac and the brothers amused for some time.

After spending time in the crowd around the stage, they had spent the next few hours wandering around the various stalls that had been set up, examining the goods, although with no real intention of spending any money that day. Instead, they filled their tankards from time to time, ate the food that had been provided, and watched the general merriment, ranging from organised traditional dancing to the more boisterous efforts of those who had drunk too freely. Isaac and the brothers knew that tomorrow would start as usual with the four o'clock bell and that William would expect hard work to make up for lost time, so they had taken things a bit easy. Isaac also had had another idea to complete his day.

About mid-afternoon, when they really didn't want to eat any more and grew tired of walking around, they were ready to make their way back to South Lynn and so they had set off, back down the High Street. It was then that Isaac had made his suggestion to the other two. "On our way back, why don't we try the *Eight Bells*. I've not been there before." If truth be told, there were many ale houses that Isaac hadn't been to yet, and his casual remark did not fool the other two for a second. After a bit of teasing, however, they had agreed to his idea, even though it wasn't really "on the way back", as they would have to go beyond the house, beyond All Saints Church, in order to reach the *Eight Bells*. But Isaac was happy.

They had found the *Eight Bells* on the corner of two lanes, about a hundred paces past the church and entered through the low doorway. It proved to be a typical ale house, with one large room with low beams and a stone floor. At the far end of the room was a large fireplace, promising warmth in the winter, but not in use on this fine day. Daylight still streamed through the windows. The room smelled of burnt tallow candles and tobacco from clay pipes.

They knew that in such an establishment they could expect to have a choice of four or five main drinks. The main one would be the traditionally brewed ale, made from fermented malt. This would be brewed on the premises and each house had its own particular brew. Then there was beer, which had the addition of hops to give it its distinctive bitter taste. This came in two main types; the best beer, at four pence a quart, and "two-penny", an inferior and weaker beer, which sold at half the price. Although not as good as the more expensive beer, it allowed a drinker to have more for his money. Some liked to drink "half-and-half", which was made up of half each of the two types of beer. Ale houses would be supplied with beer from a local brewery. The final drink that was favoured by some was "three-thread", which was a mixture of ale, best beer and "two-penny", often called "entire", or, in some places "porter"; apparently it was the favoured drink amongst the porters in the London markets. A few years back, a heavy tax had been placed on spirits, so it was unlikely that an establishment such as the *Eight Bells* would sell much by way of gin or other spirits. That was more the province of the larger public houses in the centre of town.

Since most citizens were still enjoying the revelries elsewhere, the ale house had been fairly quiet and Isaac and Nicholas made their way to a table in an alcove on the far wall. They eased themselves onto the high-backed wooden benches on either side of the beer stained table. Meanwhile, William had gone to a doorway further down the wall, which led to the small room where the casks of ale and other drinks were kept. He joined the others in a couple of minutes.

"I've ordered a large pitcher of ale. It will be here soon," he said, with a wink and a smile that Isaac recognised as meaning that he'd been up to something. Isaac looked towards the door and saw a girl approaching with the pitcher. It was the girl he had so admired in church at Easter.

Chapter Three: Courtship and Departure

That first encounter with the girl who had caught his imagination on Easter morning did not go well for Isaac. She had placed the pitcher down on the table and greeted them all cheerfully, all the time looking in Isaac's direction. The other two found this highly amusing and were making a few pointed remarks. Once more Isaac found himself blushing and a little tongue-tied. The girl laughed and walked back through the door.

In the ensuing weeks and months, Isaac, usually accompanied by the elder son, would visit the *Eight Bells* on a Saturday evening, when they knew there would be no work the following day. Gradually overcoming his initial reserve, he did manage to engage Elizabeth, for that he discovered to be her name, in brief conversation. However, she was kept busy serving the customers who frequented this particular ale house, so he never managed more than a few pleasantries, before she was off again on her duties.

One evening, whilst walking back from work in the company of his master, he decided to ask the old man's advice. After all, he was the nearest he had to a father and he couldn't get much sense from the two sons of the family. They still regarded the situation as a source of great amusement.

William gave one of his characteristic chuckles. "If you ask me," he said, "you're angling after the wrong fish." Isaac started to protest. He really had feelings for Elizabeth, he exclaimed. William put his hand on the young man's arm. "What I mean is that the girl may be pleased enough to get to know you better, but the person you really need on your side is the father. He'll be the one paying any dowry in the future, so he'll be keeping an eye on anyone who shows an interest in his daughter. Fathers can be very protective, you know. I've had three daughters of my own and they've all made good marriages with my help. Make friends with Thomas Bonner; make sure he has a good opinion of you and things will go much smoother for you. If you want, I'll come along to the *Eight Bells* with you sometime and see if I can put in a word for you."

Isaac now saw the sense in William's advice and thanked him for it. As they continued on their walk home, he felt a lot better. This new plan of action seemed to offer more hope and he now walked with a renewed spring in his step.

*   *   *   *   *

Isaac lost no time in following the old man's fatherly advice and, whenever he went to the *Eight Bells*, made a point of spending time with Thomas Bonner. He soon learnt that the family had come from Gaywood, a village a few miles from Lynn, where Thomas had worked in a local ale-house. There he had learnt the trade. His master's brother had been the owner of the *Eight Bells* at that time and, when he died without leaving an heir, Thomas had been given the chance to take over the premises. At present he was renting from his Gaywood master, but was ambitious and intended to become master in his own right as soon as he could.

The ale house was run as a family business; Thomas did most of the hard work of lifting and carrying the casks, as well as germinating and drying barley to produce the malt, whilst his wife, Susanna, was responsible for the actual brewing of the ale. Elizabeth waited on the customers and the two sons acted as pot-boys, making sure there was a constant supply of clean tankards and pitchers, as well as scrubbing down the tables and clearing up any spillages.

Thomas was not a tall man, but his muscular frame was well-developed through the constant handling of the casks of ale. The drink could flow copiously and there were often scenes of rowdiness, but Thomas was the type who would brook no nonsense, especially if it was directed towards his daughter. Many a reveller who had gone too far found himself dumped unceremoniously in the lane outside. Nevertheless, Isaac found him sociable and easy to talk to, but he also sensed that his ambitions extended to his family and wondered if he would be seen as a worthy suitor for Elizabeth.

Elizabeth herself seemed very favourably disposed towards Isaac, although he was not sure whether this was because of any genuine feeling for him, or whether it was simply how she would normally behave towards a good customer, who gave no trouble. However, he made sure that, when it was his turn to pay, he was generous in following the tradition of leaving a few extra coins for her service in fetching the pitchers of beer to the table. Isaac's usual companion on these visits was the younger William; with Nicholas still not out of his apprenticeship, he would only join them on special occasions. Although William was eleven years older than Isaac, he had taken to the younger man and enjoyed his company.

He was also ready to confide in him. On one visit, William spoke of how he saw his future and it was not to be in the sail loft.

"You may not know this, but I spent a long time completing my apprenticeship in the sail loft, as I took three years out to study surveying with a family friend in Norwich. Now I've got a chance to go and complete these studies and become qualified," he told Isaac. "I really don't want to spend all my days cooped up in the sail loft, sewing canvas. I want to be out in the fresh air more and there's so much that could be done around King's Lynn, especially to improve the harbour. That's where I see my future."

"You've obviously been thinking a lot about this," replied Isaac. "When are you planning to make this move?"

"As soon as I've broken the news to my father. I don't suppose he will be very pleased, but he must have seen it coming, with all the studying I've been doing. He probably imagined that I would take over the business from him, but it looks as though that will fall to Nicholas at some point."

"You've not told your father yet?"

"No. I'm trying to find the right moment. Now that you're qualified, it might make things a bit easier. But it still won't be that easy."

Isaac mulled over this news for a moment. He could understand his companion's wish to pursue a career more to his liking, but he also realised how it would affect the elder William. This could lead to disagreement between father and son.

"Look," Isaac finally said, "I can see your dilemma. If there's any way I can help, I will."

"Thanks. I'd really appreciate your support. If we can persuade my father to give you more responsibility at work, perhaps that will help. He does regard you now as one of the family, you know."

Isaac nodded. In some ways he was another son to William, for the old man had always wanted a bigger family. Unfortunately, the two other sons that Margaret had borne him had died young. His second son, Thomas, two years the junior of William, had died at the age of five, whilst another son, John, had survived barely a month. Whilst such deaths were not unusual in infancy, they were still a cause of much sorrow and the family still visited the graves in All Saints churchyard, even after more than twenty-five years.

But soon the conversation turned to lighter matters, including some good-natured banter from William concerning Isaac's pursuit of Elizabeth. Tomorrow would be the Sabbath, when they could rest, whilst leaving the matter of William's career until they were back at work.

                *   *   *   *   *

Back in the sail loft, a few days later, the three young men were working on a topsail. The sail had been cut to shape and the strips of canvas sewn together. Now they were preparing the seams along the edges. To help fold over the edges, they had been scored with a blunt knife-blade. Then the sail had been turned over and the folds made and pressed flat, using a wooden tool, called a seam rubber. This was basically a wedge-shaped piece of wood or whalebone, with a sharp leading edge, attached to a handle, and was used to press the seam flat prior to sewing in the boltropes along the edges of the sail.

The master of the loft was out at the moment, doing business at the quayside. Young William was still waiting for his chance to speak to him and explain his plans. Then the back door from the storeroom opened and the father returned, walking briskly towards his office. The younger William put down his tools and, glancing meaningfully in Isaac's direction, followed his father into the office. A few moments later, there were the sounds of raised voices from behind the door, followed by a quieter period. Young Nicholas looked puzzled and Isaac guessed that he had not been made privy to his brother's plans. After a few more minutes, William junior reappeared and walked back towards the others.

"Isaac," he said "My father would like a word with you." It was hard for Isaac to tell from his demeanour exactly how the interview had gone. His erstwhile drinking companion looked neither pleased nor upset. Isaac downed his tools in turn and headed for the office. He knocked and heard his master's gruff voice bidding him enter.

"Sit down, Isaac. I've something to tell you. Young William has just told me that he's off to Norwich to become a surveyor." Isaac feigned surprise. He judged that it would not be welcome for the old man to know that he was not the first to know the news. He sat in silence, not knowing how to respond.

After a moment, William spoke again. "Of course, I'm not very happy. I always expected him to follow my trade and to take over the loft when the time came. But I understand why he wants to move on and he's already spent time away from here studying his new profession. He feels he can do more in life than sew canvas and I'll not stand in his way. I admire his ambition. He'll be on the Norwich stage next week."

Isaac shifted a little uneasily on his seat. He felt that he ought to say something, but had no idea what to say. The old man, as if sensing his discomfort, started to speak again.

"Isaac, my boy, I need you to take on more responsibility around here. Nicholas is a good enough worker, but he still has two years to serve on his apprenticeship. He'll need your help to make a good finish to that."

"But I'm only just time-served myself, sir," exclaimed Isaac "Am I ready for that?"

"You may be still newly out of your time, but I can tell you now that you've learnt well the last seven years. I can trust you to pass on your knowledge to Nicholas and also to come to me if you don't know something. There may be more apprentices later this year, as well. Don't you worry, you'll be alright. And there'll be a little something extra on your salary to show for it. Without William to pay, I think I can afford it. Besides, you may be needing it, if your courting ever comes to anything." The old man gave one of his mischievous chuckles at that and Isaac found himself blushing once more. At the same time he felt a sense of relief that matters appeared to have been settled without rancour. He started to thank his master, only to be told, "Enough of that later. Now get back to work and earn your money." Isaac did as he was bid.

*   *   *   *   *

They saw little of young William that week, as he made preparations for his departure. It was left to Isaac and Nicholas to continue work on the sail, occasionally helped by their master. They managed to finish it by the Friday. As was the usual practice, William had arranged to borrow a horse and cart from the local stables and Isaac and Nicholas loaded the sail onto this and delivered it to the "Jason", a Hull packet owned by the Stockdale family of merchants, which was moored further along the quayside, near the King's Staithe.

The elder William had decided to give his son a bit of a send-off, so all four of them went to the *Eight Bells* on the Saturday evening. Even Nicholas had been allowed to join them at the ale-house, although, with his father there as well, there was little danger of him being allowed to over-indulge. The father seemed to have overcome his initial feelings of disappointment about his son's move and was in a jolly mood, regaling them with tales of his own adventures as a young man. At one time, he confessed, he had also got the wanderlust and had spent time at sea. Even there, though, he had plied his trade as a sail-maker, but was mainly employed making repairs to sails that had been damaged by high winds. There was never a chance of actually making a sail from scratch. Eventually he had grown tired of this life and had come back on shore to start his own sail loft.

Elizabeth looked after them well, fetching ale whenever their pitcher was empty. At one point during the evening, the old man went to the back room and was gone for some time. When he returned, he leaned over to Isaac and, in a low voice such that the other two could not hear, whispered, "I've just had a chat with Thomas Bonner. We got on rather well. I think he understands your prospects now." Isaac looked at his master, slightly puzzled. His look was met with a wink and a broad grin from William. Then the meaning dawned on Isaac. He was being encouraged to move things on further.

*   *   *   *   *

William junior was due to leave for Norwich on the Monday afternoon and his father had reluctantly called an early halt to work that day, so everyone could see him off. As if in sympathy with the old man's mood, the weather was wet and miserable. After starting from the centre of town, the Norwich stage would call at a coaching house that lay just on the Lynn side of the South Gate. The South Gate was part of the ancient fortifications of the town, dating back several centuries. It was an arched building that straddled the road approaching from the south. Atop the archway was a fort-like structure, with twin towers at either end, and a crenellated parapet between them. This structure offered a good vantage point to warn of any approach to the town from the south and also served as a place to collect tolls from those entering or leaving the town. Today the archway offered the family shelter from the weather as they awaited the stage.

Eventually it arrived from the direction of the town, whence it had begun its journey. Nicholas and Isaac bade farewell to their erstwhile working companion, before the senior William and his wife, Margaret, said their goodbyes. Both father and mother were obviously emotional at this parting; who knew when they might see their son again? Finally, after much embracing and hugging, the younger William was forced by the entreaties of the coachman to make ready to depart.

William had packed his clothes and a few other necessities in two large trunks, which had been hauled up onto the top of the coach. William now took his place on an outside seat, also on the top of the coach, having decided not to pay the extra required to ride inside the coach. He was probably regretting this decision already, as he pulled his heavy topcoat tighter around him to ward off the weather. It would take the coach over five hours to reach Norwich and William would not arrive there until well into the evening.

As the coach pulled away, the four remaining behind followed it through the archway and watched as it gradually disappeared into the distance. Then they turned and hurried back along the road to their home.

Later that evening, William and Margaret spent some time together, reading from one of their favourite books. This was a collection of poems by Isaac Thompson. Margaret often spent time with some of the other ladies of the town and someone had mentioned that this collection was about to be printed and would be available from a Newcastle printer by subscription, which was a common way of publishing at the time. A local printer, David Samuel, had made arrangements for copies to be sent from Newcastle on one of the colliers who regularly sailed between the two ports. Margaret had persuaded William to obtain a copy and they had duly paid their subscription. A few weeks later, their book arrived and, in the list of subscribers printed in the first few pages, were their names.

Many of the poems were of a romantic nature and William and Margaret now consoled each other for the fact that their eldest son had now left home by reading some of these to each other. Isaac had often wondered at the fact that William, who could at times be a hard task-master at the loft, also had this softer side to his character. Perhaps he had taken to heart the words of another poet, Alexander Pope, whom Thompson had quoted at the end of his preface to the collection.

Careless of censure, nor too fond of fame,
Still leased to praise, yet not afraid to blame,
Averse alike to flatter or offend,
Not free from faults, nor yet too vain to mend.

In later years, Isaac came to realise that this was a good description of William's own character and would himself try to emulate it.

*   *   *   *   *

In the days that followed William's departure, Isaac found himself preoccupied with thoughts of Elizabeth Bonner. The hours spent making sails were only interrupted on occasions by himself and Nicholas delivering the finished articles, either direct to a ship waiting at the quayside, or to the ship builders' yards for a new vessel. There were ship builders' yards both to the north and south of the town, but many vessels were towed to the Purfleet, a dock in the centre of the quaysides, by the Custom House, for final rigging and fitting out. This arrangement made it easier for all the suppliers of rigging and sails to deliver to a central location.

On these outings into the fresh air, the two young men would guide the horse and cart along the side of the river, sometimes hurrying, if the weather was inclement, or, if the day was fine and a warm sun shone on them, dawdling along and making the most of their time away from their benches. Usually, one of them would sit on the cart, holding the reins, whilst the other would actually lead the horse. They were not that confident of being able to actually drive the cart from on board and took this approach, especially when they still had their cargo of sails on board. In a way, they need not have worried, as their master took the precaution of asking the stables for one of their older, more docile, animals. He too did not wish to find their handiwork ending up in the river.

Isaac had lost his erstwhile drinking companion, but still tried to visit the *Eight Bells* each week. Sometimes his master would come along with him. Isaac found him excellent company and listened with interest to the old man's tales of his own youth in King's Lynn. By now Isaac had also made a number of acquaintances amongst the other regulars and was never short of companionship. Apart from the drinking, telling of tall tales and occasionally breaking into song, card games were quite popular. The latest fashion was Quadrille, a four-handed trick playing game, and Isaac often found himself invited into a game to make up the numbers.

All this while, the words of his master, from the night of young William's farewell evening, kept coming back to him. After a week or two, he decided it was time to make a decisive move. Thomas Bonner had left his usual post in the cask room and was clearing some tables near the door. Isaac approached. "Can I have a word, sir?" Thomas stopped, put down the empty pitchers he was holding and, indicating a chair by the table, said, "Aye, sit down, lad". Isaac did so and waited for the older man to say something more. Instead he was greeted with a raised eyebrow and a look that seemed to suggest that he was expected to open the conversation.

Isaac had rehearsed this interview quite a few times in his mind, but was now finding it difficult to know how to start. "Sir – ", he started, before pausing again. This was not easy. "Sir - I find you daughter very pleasing and would like to know her better." Once more he paused, half hoping Thomas would give him some sign of encouragement. When none came, he continued, "I would like to court your daughter. Now that I am time-served, I want to move on with my life and, if she will have me, I'd like her as my wife." These last sentences had come out as a torrent of words and Isaac now stopped, wondering if he'd overstepped the mark. He looked at Thomas in anticipation. What would his reaction be?

Thomas did not reply immediately, sitting stroking his chin, thoughtfully. After what seemed like an age to Isaac, he eventually spoke.

"I can't say I'm surprised by this. Your interest has been obvious to many of us for some time. At first I was not too pleased; you didn't seem to have the ambition to make much of yourself." Isaac's heart sank at these words, but then the older man continued. "However, your master, William, has put in a few good words on your behalf. He seems to think you will yet make something of yourself." Again he paused, but Isaac felt that a corner had been turned in the conversation and was now more hopeful. "I'll not object to you courting my daughter - in a seemly manner, mind you. Now it will be Elizabeth you'll have to convince". He smiled. "That may take you more than you've bargained for."

Isaac leapt to his feet and took Thomas's proffered hand, shaking it warmly. "Thank you, sir. I'll not disappoint you."

"Just don't disappoint my daughter. I suggest you meet us after church and offer to walk her home. You can go a few yards in front of the rest of the family and get to know each other better." Isaac readily agreed to this and left the ale house to wend his way back home, but now with a certain spring in his step.

Chapter 4: The path of true love…

Isaac took Thomas Bonner at his word and, after church the following Sunday, approached the Bonner family, as they stood chatting outside the church. Isaac thought that Elizabeth was looking particularly fine that morning, in a green dress that flowed outwards below the waist, supported as it was by whalebone hoops, and a broad-brimmed straw hat atop her bonnet. Taking off the tricorn hat he was wearing, he made an extravagant bow in front of Elizabeth, eliciting a stifled giggle from behind her fan. "Miss Elizabeth," he said, "may I walk you to your home?" She glanced towards her father, who nodded his assent, and then extended her left arm towards Isaac. He raised his right arm in order to let her rest her arm on his and they started to stroll along the church path towards the gate. Isaac was slightly dismayed to realise that the hooped skirt she wore as her best Sunday clothing made it impossible to get any closer to Elizabeth than was possible with their arms extended. The current fashion for the fan hoop, where the front and back of the hoops were drawn together by strings, made the skirt extend to the sides even further. Isaac thought that negotiating doorways must be a particular problem for the ladies.

Isaac set a leisurely pace, wishing to make the few hundred yards to the *Eight Bells* last as long as possible. He decided that he would try to find out more about Elizabeth, so he asked about her life in Gaywood, before they moved to South Lynn. Although Gaywood was less than two miles from the centre of King's Lynn, Isaac had never had occasion to visit there. Elizabeth described a small community, consisting of a church, a few cottages, the ale house where her father worked, and a number of windmills. These latter had been her abiding memory from her childhood and she had always been fascinated by these strange buildings, with their sails turning in the wind. On occasion, she had been allowed inside and witnessed the corn being ground beneath large stone wheels to produce the flour for everyone's staple food; bread.

All too soon they had arrived at the ale house and could only exchange a few more words, before the rest of the Bonner family, who had been following some thirty paces behind them, arrived. Once more Isaac removed his hat and bowed to Elizabeth, thanking her for her company. She, in turn thanked him and Isaac felt that this first real chance to engage her in meaningful conversation had gone well. Although he had often spoken to her in the ale house, it had always been in the company of other drinkers and she had always been too busy to exchange more than a few pleasantries. He said his farewells to the rest of the family and walked back to the Elstobb home, a happy man.

This pattern was followed on most Sundays and the pair learnt a lot about each other through these conversations. There were even times at the ale house when Isaac could get to speak with Elizabeth alone, without the rest of the family watching their every move. They would go out to the back of the ale house to a room where barley was processed into malt. The drying process kept this room very warm and Isaac enjoyed the pungent aroma of the drying malt. It was on one of these occasions that Isaac suffered a bit of a set back, at least in his own mind. Isaac had started by wondering where they would be in twenty years time. He himself said that he expected to be a master sail-maker with his own sail loft. He would be married and would probably be teaching at least one of his sons his trade. When it came to Elizabeth's turn, however, it seemed that she didn't share this vision of the future. Her dream was that, some time soon, one of the gentry would visit the ale house, take a liking to her and raise her station in life by marrying her. Isaac was disappointed to hear this. He thought to himself that this was unlikely to happen, as the *Eight Bells* was not an ale house likely to attract the gentry; they would be more likely to be found at the larger establishments in the centre of town, like the *Duke's Head*. In any case, he felt that they would treat an alehouse keeper's daughter more as a source of sport, rather than any serious relationship. However, he kept this thought to himself and became more determined to bring Elizabeth round to his way of thinking. But he could see that this was not set to be a whirlwind romance, but would take some time.

*   *   *   *   *

Autumn was giving way to winter. The harvests had been gathered and the Harvest Home celebrated in All Saints. It had been a good harvest this year and there would be plenty of bread available during the winter months. Meat was also in good supply at a reasonable price, as this was the time of year that the farmers in the neighbouring countryside reduced their stock, to avoid having to spend too much on feed. The butchers' stalls at the markets were doing brisk business, as were the salt merchants, whose product was needed for the main method used to preserve the meat. Another was smoking, a method much favoured for the fish that was plentiful in the area.

The pattern of the working day was also changing. As the hours of daylight grew fewer, the morning bell, that rang from the church tower to arouse the populace for their daily toil, now tolled an hour later. At the sail loft, work was confined to the hours of daylight. William Elstobb saw no need to add to his expenses by burning candles or lighting oil lamps. Most of the work consisted of repairs to sails damaged in the autumn gales and what little work there was on new sails was not against particular orders, but to have a stock of the most commonly required types ready for the spring, when the shipyards would increase their production again.

Isaac still managed to visit the *Eight Bells* a few times a week after work. At least there he could be assured of a welcoming fire and some light to see by. If William did not supply many candles at the loft, he was equally frugal in his own home and encouraged the household to retire to their beds as soon as any household chores had been completed. In the ale house, Isaac could have a drink, play cards, or sing a few songs with his companions. And, of course, he could try to have brief conversations with Elizabeth. Although they still enjoyed a walk together after church, the changing weather did not encourage them to linger too long, so they often reached the ale house having said very little. Isaac was still not sure whether their dreams of the future were any closer to becoming the same.

One evening, Isaac was sitting by himself, slowly supping a tankard of ale, when Thomas Bonner came and sat with him.

"How are things going between you and our Elizabeth?"

Isaac was a little taken aback by Thomas's forthright manner, but tried to answer as best he could.

"I'm not too sure – you see, when I talk of my future being that of a married man, with my own business and bringing up a family, she seems to have other ideas…" He trailed off, not quite knowing how to explain things. After a moment the older man tried to prompt him into saying more.

"How do you mean – other ideas?"

"She has this notion that some member of the gentry will come into your ale house, take a fancy to her and take her away from all this."

"Aye, lad – she was always a bit fanciful. Too much of a dreamer, I'd say. She needs to realise what is more likely to happen to her. If she holds out for her ideal man, she's likely to end up an old maid. We just don't get the gentry in here – not in South Lynn, not in a simple ale house!"

"But what's to be done about it?"

"You must keep trying, lad. My wife, Susanna, and I will press your suit as best we may, but may be best if we don't seem to push her too hard – Elizabeth can be a bit stubborn at times. Let's see what the next few months bring. Just don't give up." He paused for a moment, before adding, "I've an idea. Just wait there a moment."

At that, Thomas got up and went to the back room. Isaac thought hard about what he had said, as he finished his ale. He was encouraged by the support he was getting and vowed that he would, indeed, not give up the chase.

After some ten minutes, Thomas came back with a freshly sealed letter. "Give this to your master, when you get home. It may help." Despite

Isaac's puzzled look, he did not say anything further, but returned once more to the back room.

Isaac left and made his way back to his master's house. It was a clear, frosty night and he was aided by a near full moon, so he didn't bother to take one of the rush torches left outside the ale house for the benefit of the customers. When he arrived back, he found that William was sitting in the main room by the dying embers of the fire. Everyone else must have already gone to their beds. Isaac passed the letter over to the old man, who broke the seal and, straining to make out the message therein by the light of the few candles that were still lit, read it. Eventually he lowered the letter and turned to Isaac.

"It seems that we have all, as a family, been invited to share a Christmas meal with the Bonners at the *Eight Bells*. Thomas particularly mentions you in the letter. I think that, when you next go round the market, you should be keeping an eye out for some suitable presents to take with you, especially for anyone you might be trying to impress."

He gave one of his chuckles and winked broadly.

"I will write back our acceptance of this kind invitation. We can also invite them here, perhaps for Twelfth Night. Now I suggest you get to your bed. It's still a work day tomorrow, you know."

*   *   *   *   *

It was Christmas morning and the two families met outside the door of All Saints, after the morning service. The Bonners were Thomas, Susanna, Elizabeth and the two boys, John and Edward, whilst William junior had returned from Norwich to spend the Christmas period with the Elstobb family. They exchanged their Christmas greetings and the usual pleasantries, before setting off together for the *Eight Bells*. Isaac, as was now his usual practice, supporting Elizabeth's arm as he walked alongside her. When they reached the ale house, Thomas led them through a side door and into the main living room, which served as somewhere to sit, a kitchen and a dining room. In the centre of the room was a large table, with places set for ten. A glorious smell emanated from the direction of the fireplace at the end of the room. Susanna Bonner had been preparing for their Christmas dinner from early morning, leaving various items cooking, whilst they were at church.

Thomas poured some strong barley wine into glasses and distributed them amongst the menfolk. Elizabeth, Margaret and the young boys drank small beer, whilst Susanna busied herself checking the progress of the meal. They chattered happily amongst themselves. This was the first time that all the family members had had the chance to socialise properly. Naturally, Thomas was familiar with Isaac and the male members of the Elstobb family, from their visits to the *Eight Bells* as customers, as was also Elizabeth. The two families had also spent time talking after church each week, but now they were all together sharing a meal.

Eventually, Susanna declared that all was ready and called for them to take their places at the table. Thomas indicated where each should sit. He sat at one end of the table, with William to his right and Isaac to his left. Elizabeth was sat next to Isaac and Margaret by her husband. William junior sat next to his mother and then John, whilst, on the other side, Edward was alongside his sister, Nicholas came next and Susanna's place was at the far end of the table, nearest the fire. And so started their feast.

This was indeed a feast, destined to last several hours and leave them all feeling very full. First was served a fine soup made with peas and ham, served with spiced bread. Then they were regaled with a selection of meats and fish, with the centrepiece being two large geese. The area around King's Lynn and further into Norfolk was renowned for the rearing of geese. Most of the geese had left the county some three months back and been driven in huge flocks along the roads to London, but this pair had been kept back and had spent recent weeks in the garden at the back of the *Eight Bells*. There was also a fine joint of beef sirloin, some mutton, a large dish of pilchards, as well as various pies and hams. They were accompanied by potatoes and other root vegetables, and washed down with more barley wine, ale and beer. The meal concluded with a large boiled pudding, flavoured with raisins and other fruits. All agreed that it had been a splendid meal and thanked their host and his wife for their generosity.

Then came the time to exchange gifts. Since finishing his apprenticeship, Isaac had enjoyed the extra income he now received, but had not let it change his ways too much. He had had to be careful with money for the last seven years and, apart from a few luxuries, like a better wig, a few items of clothing and some new shoes, had not made any large purchases. As a result he had saved a fair amount, so he could afford to buy reasonable presents for the first time. Mostly, these were fairly commonplace items; some tobacco for the two senior men, handkerchiefs for their wives, some worsted stockings for the Elstobb brothers and wooden ball and cup games for the younger boys. But, of course, his present to Elizabeth was the one he had agonised over the longest. It was wrapped in tissue paper, so she could not see it until she removed this paper. Then she gave a squeal of delight. Isaac's present was a pair of elbow length, white kid gloves. He had also found a seamstress in the town to embroider a letter "E" on the back of each hand in silk thread.

"Oh, these are lovely," she exclaimed with delight, "Thank you, Isaac, thank you so much!" With that she gave him a hug and a kiss on each cheek. Thomas and William exchanged glances and smiled contentedly.

"And I've something for you," said Elizabeth, handing a packet to Isaac. He opened it and found inside a dark green cravat.

"Why thank you, Elizabeth," Isaac said. This had come as a bit of a surprise, little guessing at the prompting that had gone on in the Bonner household, or the efforts of Susanna in making sure Elizabeth had the chance to visit the market. "I shall keep this to wear with my best clothes." Once more they exchanged a hug and chaste kisses.

Then the party split into two, with the men sitting round the fire with their ale and their clay pipes, whilst the ladies stayed at the table chatting. The two young boys were soon challenging each other to see who was the more skilful with the cup and ball game. The talk and drinking went on late into the evening and all felt that this had been a most enjoyable Christmas Day.

* * * * *

On their next stroll back from the church after Sunday service, both Isaac and Elizabeth were pleased to notice that the other was wearing the Christmas gifts they had exchanged. Isaac took this for a sign that matters had taken a turn for the better and was emboldened by it.

"Elizabeth," he said nervously, "can I ask you something?"

"Oh, this sounds serious. Do go on."

He paused a moment, before continuing. "Well – in a few weeks it will be the Mart." King's Lynn had held a fair, known as the Mart, early each February, following the Feast of the Virgin, for three hundred years. "Could you get the time off from the ale house to accompany me to the Mart? I mean, do you think your father will approve?"

Elizabeth gave one of her little laughs and said, "We will have to ask him. But do you think I could trust you?"

Isaac started to explain that his intentions towards her were entirely honourable, but soon realised that she was laughing again and this time is was at his discomfiture. She interrupted his protestations and, with a smile, said, "I'm sure my father will have no objections. For some reason, he seems to like you…"

By now, they had reached the *Eight Bells* and stood at the door for a moment, waiting for the remainder of the two families to catch up, before they all went in for a quiet drink and a chat.

* * * * *

There had indeed been no problem in Elizabeth having the time away from the ale house to go to the Mart. Isaac and Elizabeth knew that the Mart would not start until mid-say on the opening day and, even then, there would be time taken up with ceremony, as the Mayor made his official speech to commence the celebrations. They decided, therefore, to go on the second day of the Mart, Saturday the fourth of February, to give themselves more time, as Elizabeth still had to be back at the *Eight Bells* before night fall. She would be needed to wait on tables that evening. Isaac called at the *Eight Bells* as early as he could, with the winter sun still low in the sky. It was a cold, bright, and frosty morning and both he and Elizabeth were wrapped in their winter clothing, with thick topcoats. Although neither of them wore their Sunday clothes, Isaac noticed once more that Elizabeth was wearing the gloves he had given her.

They walked quickly from South Lynn across into the main town and on to the Tuesday Market Place, where the Mart was traditionally held. Already activities were in full swing and there was a good number of citizens in the square.

Being an annual fair and one of the largest in this part of England, as well as being the first one in the area after the Christmas period, it had attracted many more merchants than would normally be there for the weekly market. Stalls were crowded into the square, which, although large, could not hold them all and some spilled into neighbouring streets and lanes. As Isaac and Elizabeth strolled amongst the rows of stalls, they found that merchants had come from far and wide to be there. As well as the local accent, with which they were familiar, there were others that they could not place, as well as a fair number of stallholders who barely spoke any English, being mainly from the Low Countries. The stallage paid by all these merchants, plus any tolls levied on the goods they were selling, brought a good income to the town, although local stallholders were charged at half the rate of strangers.

Elizabeth was quite happy inspecting the various goods on offer, occasionally lingering over something that particularly took her fancy. Isaac tried to note the sorts of item that would please her, in case he could turn this to his advantage. They would occasionally stop to watch itinerant entertainers showing their skills; jugglers, fire-eaters, all manner of trained animal performing tricks and so on. At the prompting of Elizabeth, Isaac rewarded some of the better acts with a few coins.

It was around mid-day when they encountered Nicholas. At his suggestion they decided to take a break for some refreshment and went and sat at a table outside the *Angel* for a drink of beer and a small meal of bread and cheese. Isaac guessed, quite correctly, that Nicholas wanted them to join him, as he was less likely to be challenged about drinking at a public house while still an apprentice. They sat and chatted happily for some time, with Isaac and Nicholas regaling Elizabeth with tales of life in the sail loft. Over the years there had many amusing incidents involving old William, Isaac and the two brothers and Elizabeth laughed heartily at some of their tales. After a while, Isaac excused himself for a moment and left the table. He managed to slip back among the stalls without Elizabeth noticing, where he made a purchase at one to which he had noticed Elizabeth paying particular attention earlier in the day. He was gone but a short while and Elizabeth had assumed it was a call of nature. Isaac was not about to set her right just yet. After their lunch, Isaac and Elizabeth parted once more from Nicholas and returned to the fair, wandering further among the stalls and enjoying the street entertainment for another hour and a half. Then they started on their way back to the *Eight Bells*. On the journey back they passed close to All Saints church.

"A moment, please, Elizabeth. Will you walk with me through the churchyard." In the churchyard, there were a number of large trees, now standing bare of foliage, and Isaac led Elizabeth to one of these, which offered them some respite from the cold breeze. Pulling a small packet from under his coat, he presented it to her.

"I'd like you to have this present. It's a piece of Flemish lace. I think it would be a lovely thing to trim a dress – perhaps a wedding dress. I'd like to see you back in this church in such a dress." He dropped to one knee and took hold of her hand. "Elizabeth, please will you do me the honour of becoming my wife? Will you marry me?"

Chapter Five: Changes

It seemed an eternity to Isaac before Elizabeth spoke. As he knelt before her, looking up anxiously, all he heard were the ever-present cries of the gulls over the river and the sound of the wind in the branches above. He held on to her hand and waited anxiously for her answer. In reality, it was only a few seconds before she spoke.

"Dear Isaac, you have been so kind to me for so long. I realise that I want to be with you for ever. Of course I'll marry you."

At this, Isaac sprang to his feet and gathered Elizabeth into his arms. They kissed each other; not the chaste kisses on the cheek they had enjoyed up to that time, but, for the first time, a truly passionate embrace. They both forgot the chill of the February day that was drawing towards eventide, as they seemed to enter a world of their own. They hugged and kissed for a long time in the gathering gloom, before Elizabeth spoke.

"Isaac, my love, it's getting quite dark now – we need to go. Let us go and share our news with the family – I'm sure they will be pleased for us."

They set off along the route they had followed many a time after church, hurrying towards the ale house. When they arrived, it was Elizabeth who broke the news to her parents and, as anticipated, they were overjoyed to hear it. Whilst her mother hugged her, Thomas took Isaac to one side.

"Well done, lad!" he cried, slapping Isaac on the back, "Let's drink to the future!" At that, he fetched a bottle of his best barley wine and some glasses. Soon they had all started a started a series of toasts to the newly engaged couple, which were enthusiastically returned, as Isaac and Elizabeth thanked Thomas and Susanna for all they had done to smooth the path of their romance.

It was more than an hour later that a very happy Isaac left for home, glowing from the effects of the wine and from a sense of exultation at his acceptance by Elizabeth. Soon he was enjoying a fresh round of congratulations from the Elstobb family. Despite the effects of the wine and the beer that William had pressed upon him, Isaac was to find it hard to sleep that night, as he tried to relive every moment of that special day.

*   *   *   *   *

Isaac little thought at this time how long it would be before his marriage to Elizabeth. As it was to turn out, it would be over two years before they were able to wed. They would need somewhere to live, together with furniture, and to save for this would take time. There would be other events along the way that would have an influence on how matters would be resolved. But Isaac did not think of such things at this time. He had become engaged to the girl he loved and that was all that mattered.

He now spent a lot of time at the *Eight Bells*; even more than before. But it was not the ale or the company of other customers that was now the attraction. He was well aware of his need to save money. Instead, he spent more time in the family's rooms away from the drinking parlour, getting to know more about his new fiancée and her family. On occasions, with the blessing of Thomas and Susanna, the couple would indulge in the common custom of the time of "bundling". They would be left alone in Elizabeth's room and on her bed, dressed in little more than night clothes, to kiss and cuddle each other, although Susanna would always make sure that her daughter's shift was firmly tied at the bottom, to prevent anything more than this. Despite his frustration, Isaac found these sessions alone with Elizabeth much to his liking. They were able to find out more about each other and to have long conversations; much longer than the ones they had enjoyed in their walks back from the church.

At work, William had taken on another apprentice shortly after Isaac had finished his term. This was Mathew Fisher, the son of a weaver from a small town, Wells-next-the-Sea, which was about twenty-five miles from King's Lynn along the north Norfolk coast. Wells-next-the Sea was a fairly busy port and William had built up contacts with merchants and ships' masters there, to supply them with sails. It was through one of these contacts that Mathew had been recommended to him.

Isaac found Mathew pleasant enough, but, with him being only fourteen years of age, they had little in common to converse about. William, however, expected Isaac to instruct Mathew in the skills of the trade, so they spent a lot of time together at work. Both Isaac and Nicholas welcomed the newcomer in one sense, as he would be the one given some of the less welcome tasks about the loft. It was good to have someone more junior to lift them in the hierarchy.

Nicholas's own apprenticeship finished in the summer of 1738 and William again took the opportunity to take on another apprentice. Once more his contact at Wells-next-the-Sea supplied a suitable candidate, one Stephen Magnus. Both Stephen and Mathew lived in the Elstobb household, sharing William junior's old room. As Isaac was kept busy with Mathew, the task of overseeing Stephen's training fell to Nicholas.

As 1738 moved from summer to autumn, events were to occur that were to have a profound effect on Isaac's life and change his plans for the future.

*   *   *   *   *

One evening in October, William had asked Isaac to join him and Nicholas for a drink after work. Unusually, he had decided not to go to the *Eight Bells*, but chose to walk northwards along the quay, before heading inland at the Custom House towards the *Prince of Wales* public house in Purfleet Street. Soon the trio were sitting in an alcove with their tankards of ale.

Once they were settled, William started to speak. "Isaac, I have been having a few thoughts lately and have discussed these with young Nicholas here." He paused, leaving Isaac to wonder what was to come. William continued, "As you know, I am not a young man – I'm sixty-seven now and beginning to feel it. I've spent too many years cooped up in the loft and I would like to spend more time with Margaret. I've decided to step back from running the loft and hand it over to Nicholas. It will be his business now."

Isaac took a moment to absorb this news. It was inevitable that one of the sons would inherit the business and, with William junior's change of career, that responsibility naturally fell on Nicholas. But he had not expected it quite so soon. One question was uppermost in his mind.

"But what will this mean for me? Have I to move out, or what?"

"Don't worry, lad. Your job is safe for now. Nicholas will need your help, especially to keep an eye on young Mathew and Stephen. But sooner or later, he'll want to be his own man and will decide for himself how to run things. If I were you, I would be looking at how you could branch out on your own in a few years and have your own loft. The merchants are adding new ships to the fleet all the time, so there'll be plenty of custom for another loft. You do good work and will have no problem attracting custom. If you think ahead now, it will be easier. If you see any tools or other equipment for sale, I'd buy them. You can store them at the loft until you're ready to move on."

"Yes," interjected Nicholas, "I want you to stay on at the loft for quite some time – at least until the two youngsters become useful, although that won't be for another five or six years. But you'll want to be your own master eventually, so we'll give you every help."

Isaac had not been expecting all this, but he could see the logic behind it. William's advice to prepare by acquiring the necessary equipment was good, although it might place further strain on his finances at a time when he needed to save for his wedding. He would have to tell Elizabeth that they might need to wait a bit longer. After a short period of silence while he was turning all this over in his mind, he looked up at the other two and raised his tankard.

"Here's health to the old Master and a long and happy retirement, and here's health to the new Master. May the business continue to prosper in your hands."

Father and son returned the toast, wishing Isaac all the best in the future. Indeed, they continued toasting each other for some time, so that by the time they left and set off on the walk home, all of them were a little unsteady on their feet, as they picked their way along the darkened streets, by the light of a rush torch. But, half an hour later, they did reach their house, to be greeted by one of Margaret's sturdy broths and large chunks of bread. Once again, Isaac had much to mull over, as he lay on his bed later.

*   *   *   *   *

As expected, Isaac's next meeting with Elizabeth was a bit awkward. They had been planning for a spring wedding, but now it was likely that this would prove to be impracticable. They discussed all the possibilities at length. Elizabeth suggested that her father might help. Although Thomas would not be able to afford a large dowry, Elizabeth felt that what he would be able to give them would at least help them to set up a home and they would have to be content with renting quite a cheap place, at least in the beginning. Eventually they decided to delay a few months and marry in the summer of 1739. This would give Isaac more time to find somewhere to live and buy the essential items of furniture and household goods they would need. This settled, they could resume the more pleasurable activity of "bundling".

Chapter Six: O Happy Day!

11th August 1739. It was a bright Saturday morning at the height of summer, when Isaac rose early and dressed in his best clothes, complete with his favourite cravat; the one Elizabeth had given him at that first Christmas feast together. He looked around his room, which seemed very bare and empty. This was because most of his belongings had already been moved to the cottage in town that was to be their new home. What little was left would be taken with them later that day.

After a breakfast of bacon and bread, he set out for All Saints Church shortly after eight o'clock, full of joy and anxious expectation. This was his wedding day. Nicholas and William junior were to act as his groomsmen and accompanied him on his walk, attempting to keep his nerves in check with a stream of banter and jokes, most of them at his expense and often ribald. They soon arrived at the church and found a good crowd of friends and well-wishers awaiting them. Old William was there with Margaret and the two apprentices, Mathew and Stephen. Susanna Bonner and her two sons were also waiting; Thomas would be accompanying his daughter to the church a bit later. Isaac spent a short time moving amongst the small crowd, chatting briefly with as many as he could and thanking them for their good wishes, before Nicholas caught up with him and suggested they move inside. Isaac, William junior and Nicholas led the way in and moved to the front row of pews. Isaac had never been this far forward in the church before and, as he sat waiting for the service to begin, looked around him at parts of the church architecture he had not been able to see in such detail from the pew near the back. The body of the church was separated from the chancel by a screen. The chancel itself was an area reserved for the clergy, whilst the congregation were usually in the nave of the church, where the priest would conduct services from the pulpit. Being so close to the chancel screen, Isaac could now see that this screen was decorated by paintings of the apostles. These were quite dark in appearance, covered as they were by the grime they had collected in the centuries since they were first painted. With the front pews so close to the chancel arch, the Rood, or large crucifix, with a statue of the crucified Christ, was almost over the top of Isaac's head.

Whilst Isaac was thus waiting ready in the church, Elizabeth was leaving the *Eight Bells* for her short journey to her wedding, on the arm of her father. The previous evening, the Bonner family and friends had collected all the chipped and broken crockery and smashed it outside the door, so that Elizabeth's first steps on leaving the ale house were over a path of broken crockery. This tradition was thought to bring good luck to her in her new life.

Back in the church, the vicar, the Reverend Pyle, had made his entry from the vestry and taken up his position in the centre of the aisle, just in front of the front pews. Then the church door was heard to open and the congregation rose to their feet. Isaac couldn't resist the urge to turn round and saw his bride-to-be walking down the aisle towards him, her proud father by her side and two close friends walked behind as her bridesmaids. She was wearing a pale blue dress and, as she grew nearer, Isaac noticed that the collar of the dress was trimmed with lace; the very piece of lace that he had presented to her at time of his proposal. Her head was adorned with a garland of flowers and she was smiling happily. Isaac thought she had never looked so beautiful. As she arrived in front of the vicar, Isaac moved alongside her. Then the service began, with the vicar intoning the familiar words of the traditional form of Matrimony in the Book of Common Prayer.

"Dearly beloved, we are gathered together here in the sight of God, and in the face of this Congregation, to join together this man and this woman in holy Matrimony…"

For Isaac, the service passed almost as in a dream. When they reached the point of exchanging their vows, he turned towards Elizabeth and looked deep into her eyes, as he repeated the words after the Reverend Pyle. At last it was time to put the wedding ring on her finger. They had chosen together a gold poesy ring, which outwardly was a plain band, but inside the ring was inscribed "Time shall tell I love you". Such rings, bearing similar sentiments, had been very popular in times past and, although perhaps a little old-fashioned now, both Elizabeth and Isaac had been pleased to find this one on sale at the Tuesday Market Place. It had been a bit expensive, but they both had fallen for the sentiment inscribed therein and had agreed on this extravagance.

After blessing the newly married couple, the vicar announced the singing of Psalm 128: *Beati Omnes* "Blessed are they that fear the Lord", which was sung with gusto by the assembly of the families and the many friends who had also come to witness the marriage service. The rest of the service passed by in a whirl. Isaac and Elizabeth sat together as the vicar preached his sermon on their duties as a married couple, but, so intent on each other were they, that they hardly heard him. After taking communion together, kneeling at the low rail in front of the screen, they were at last able to walk down the aisle together as man and wife and emerge into the warm summer sun, where they were soon joined by the rest of their families and friends. As they stood on the steps of the church, a peal of bells rang out from the tower above and they both felt that they had never been happier. Having received the congratulations of friends and family, it was time for the walk back to the *Eight Bells*, where the wedding feast was prepared.

It was a merry party that made their way back to the ale house, with the newlyweds in the lead, flanked by the groomsmen and bridesmaids, followed by the rest of the celebrating crowd. When they arrived, wheat grains were thrown over them and in their path, as a traditional way of wishing them fertility. Then they all crowded inside. As well as the Bonners and the Elstobbs, many of the regular customers from the ale house and other neighbours and friends were there for the wedding feast. This had been prepared by Susanna and Margaret, and rivalled any of the Christmas meals that the families had enjoyed together in the past three winters. The table in the Bonners' main room was laden with good fare; there were roast geese and other fowl, beef, ham and fresh fish. Of course, Thomas had also made sure that there would be plenty to drink.

Isaac took off his jacket, fastened one of Thomas's aprons around his waist and began to distribute tankards of ale around the tables in the main drinking parlour. Thomas carved the various meats and Susanna and Margaret distributed these among the happy guests. Soon everyone was enjoying the food and drink, chatting happily and toasting the happy couple.

As time wore on and the ale took effect, many of the company took to singing. The songs were traditional songs that had been sung down the centuries, with some of them being quite bawdy, giving the newlyweds encouragement and advice for later that night. These were accompanied by one of the guests on a fiddle and soon the dancing began. Isaac was expected to take a turn around the floor with all the young ladies present, still with the encouragement of the singers in the room:

> *He dances all the maidens o'er*
> *Then rubs his face and makes a bow*
> *So marches off, what can he do?*
> *He must not tire himself outright*
> *The bride expects a dance at night!*

Later it was to be Elizabeth's turn to dance, in the traditional dance of the bridal crown. During this dance, she was surrounded by the married women, who circled around her, symbolically protecting her virtue. It was left to the two groomsmen, William and Nicholas, to break this circle and steal the wreath of flowers from her head. This was then broken and scattered on the floor, which resulted in a mad scramble from the single girls; it was a long held superstition that if a piece of the broken wreath was taken home, the lucky girl would be married within a year. Another superstition accompanied the serving of the "bride's pie", a pie filled with minced meat and sweetbreads. The single girls were fed with a small piece of the pie that had been passed through Elizabeth's wedding ring, which was believed to bring them good fortune in finding a husband. There was also a glass ring hidden in the pie and whoever found this was expected to be the next to marry.

Towards the end of the celebrations at the Eight Bells, old William read an extract from one of the poem's in his favourite book, the one by Isaac Thompson.

And be you Parents of a num'rous Race,
Enrich'd with ev'ry Good and ev'ry Grace;
Whose Wit, and Charms, and Innocence, and Truth,
May be true Copies of their Parents' Youth;
And may your Happiness augment from theirs,
Joy of your Age, and Comfort of your Years;
'Till peaceful Slumbers close at last your Eyes,
And call you from the Earth, to mount the Skies.

As William finished, the company applauded loudly and echoed the sentiments of the poem, toasting the happy couple once more and wishing them a fruitful union.

The celebrations had started on their return from church at about eleven o'clock and were to continue into the evening, before it was time to move on to Isaac and Elizabeth's new home. They were to be taken there in a carriage, kindly lent for the occasion by one of the loft's customers, whilst the families and a few more friends crowded into a hay wagon that had been borrowed. Both carriage and wagon were decorated overall with garlands of flowers. The boisterous party set off for the centre of King's Lynn.

The same merchant who had lent them the carriage also owned property in the town and Isaac had agreed to rent a cottage in Priory Lane, just off Lath Street and running alongside St Margaret's Church. It was a small place, in a row of similar buildings; just one main room downstairs and one bedroom. Isaac had scoured the market for some basic furniture. He had bought a good four poster bed, which had had to be taken apart to get it up the narrow stairs and then reassembled. Also in the bedroom there was a large coffer, for storage, a chair, and a wash-stand. The main room down stairs was equally sparsely furnished. The main feature was a good-sized stone fireplace, with a small oven and hob alongside. Isaac had found four wooden chairs, two with arms, and a table, as well as a dresser. It wasn't much and was all second hand, but this, along with other basic items, would have to do for the start of their life together.

The wedding party disembarked from their transport outside the cottage, carrying quite a few bottles of ale, together with bread and cold cuts of meat. This party was yet to run its course. The carriage and cart drove off to be returned to their owners.

Once inside the cottage, Elizabeth removed her garters and hung them on the groomsmen's hats, before being ushered upstairs by Susannah, Margaret and the two bridesmaids. Then William junior and Nicholas helped Isaac out of his clothes and into his nightshirt, before sitting him down with an ale to await events. After a short while, a call from upstairs indicated that all was ready and the men climbed the narrow staircase to the bedroom.

Elizabeth was already in the bed when they arrived. Isaac removed his stockings and climbed into the bed beside her. The groomsmen took Elizabeth's stockings from where they lay on the bed, whilst the bridesmaids picked up Isaac's. Then the four of them sat at the foot of the bed, facing away from the newlyweds, and threw the stockings over their heads. To much applause and laughter, two of the stockings landed squarely on the heads of Isaac and Elizabeth, a sure sign that the throwers would themselves soon be married. Then all the party left the room to go downstairs, leaving Isaac and Elizabeth alone at last. For the guests, this would not be the end of the revelries, as they sang, ate and drank their supplies, and shouted various pieces of advice, or ribald speculation, up to the happy couple. The company downstairs would eventually fall asleep downstairs, not wishing to make the walk back to South Lynn until after daybreak. Meanwhile, Isaac and Elizabeth held each other close and began their married life in the manner that all expected.

Chapter Seven: Mixed Fortunes

Isaac had settled well into his new position as a married man and was enjoying life with Elizabeth. The move to nearer the centre of King's Lynn had brought with it many advantages, as well as some drawbacks. Now he was much closer to his work. The back of the cottage opened into a small courtyard, which connected to Lath Street through an opening in the houses on the east side of Lath Street. Isaac could leave by the back door, cross the courtyard, and then go out onto Lath Street. He then turned to the left and walked fifty paces along the road, before crossing into the alleyway that led to the loft. He could be there in two minutes. This meant that he could rise from his bed later and enjoy a good breakfast before setting out. For Elizabeth too, things were more convenient. Turning right from Priory Lane and continuing onto St Margaret's Way, past the church, it was around two hundred yards to the Saturday Market Place. True, it was a much longer walk to the Tuesday Market Place, but nowhere near the distance they had had to walk from South Lynn.

The streets were also better here than in South Lynn. The major roads were paved with cobblestones, which, although greatly in need of repair, were better than South Lynn's narrow tracks. They were also wide enough for two carriages to pass each other. On the other hand, there was also a greater amount of traffic, whether it was single riders or carriages, and one needed to watch one's step, to avoid the horse droppings that were evident everywhere. Each street also had one or two ditches flanking it, which served as a conduit for waste matter, both human and animal. At times the stench, especially in high summer, could be overpowering. Closer to home, there was a cesspit on the other side of the courtyard at the back of the cottage, where they could dispose of their night-soil and contents of the earth closet situated by the back door. The cesspit was emptied periodically by a man with a cart and the contents taken away to the countryside. Unlike South Lynn, where water had to be fetched from wells or one of the river inlets, known as fleets, the town was supplied with water along a system of pipes. The water was drawn mainly from the Gaywood River and then pumped by a mill into storage tanks, built on the town walls in the previous century. From these so-called kettle mills, it was distributed by pipes, using gravity. Unfortunately, these pipes were prone to leakage and contamination, so the actual supply could prove to be inadequate. It was necessary to have a water butt for extra storage, which was topped up by rainwater, or by drawing water from the fleets. Another hazard, being near the river, was that of flooding. As well as the damage this frequently caused, it also drove vermin inland. Rats were a constant problem and the ratcatcher and his dog were kept busy.

On balance, however, both Isaac and Elizabeth agreed that their life was much improved and they were happy together. Money was still short, as Isaac continued with his dream of having his own sail loft, as well as their shared dream of starting a family.

*   *   *   *   *

At the sail loft, work continued as usual. They were kept busy with orders, both for repairs and new sails. The two apprentices continued to improve and took a greater share of the work now. Isaac had noticed a change in Nicholas, however. Since his coming of age, he had decided to join the Society of Friends, or Quakers. There had been a number on nonconformist sects founded in Lynn over the last century and the Friends were amongst the oldest of these. Initially, these sects had suffered persecution, but had now become accepted in the main, although their practices and beliefs remained a cause for suspicion amongst the majority of the population, who still followed the ways of the established Church. Nicholas had obviously done well within the Friends, as he conducted business for them, such as arranging the purchase or lease of land to be used as burial grounds. Isaac didn't see as much of Nicholas now in a social environment, possibly because of the Quakers views on strong drink, but he also suspected that this might be because Nicholas also had a romantic interest in one of his fellow Quakers.

The months passed and there was still no sign of Isaac and Elizabeth starting a family. They had been married for over a year, before

Elizabeth began to notice signs that perhaps things were about to change. At first she confided only in Isaac and asked him to keep it as a secret between them, but, by the time Christmas was approaching, it was unmistakable; she was expecting their first-born. The happy news was given to the rest of the family at the festive gathering on Christmas Day at the *Eight Bells*. Thomas and Susanna were overjoyed, as they had also been waiting impatiently for a grandchild. That year's celebrations had an extra verve to them.

One Monday in early May, a boy appeared at the door of the loft with a message for Isaac. Elizabeth had gone into labour. As the day's work was already drawing to a close he left at once, pausing only to ask Nicholas to call in at the *Eight Bells* and tell Thomas and Susanna the news. The he hurried out of the building and headed up the alley to the street. Before continuing home, he knocked at a door of a house near the entrance to the cottages, since there was a midwife there, called Charity Smith, who had agreed to help when the time came. She quickly picked up a bag, in which she had whatever she might need, and the two of them hurried to the cottage.

By the time they arrived, Elizabeth was already upstairs on the bed. Isaac was only allowed to stay briefly by the bedside, before Charity ushered him away downstairs, with instructions to put a pan of water on the hob. Once this had heated, Charity collected it and took it upstairs, leaving Isaac to wait anxiously downstairs. He could hear Elizabeth crying out in pain from their bedroom, but had to remain, feeling rather helpless, sometimes sitting in one of the chairs by the hearth-side, sometimes pacing the stone floor.

After about an hour, Susanna arrived. She tried to offer Isaac some comfort. She reminded him that she herself had been through childbirth three times and assured him that, whatever the pains of labour Elizabeth had to suffer, it would ultimately be worth it. Then she also went upstairs, leaving Isaac alone with his thoughts. It was left to Nicholas, who arrived a short time later, to come and keep Isaac company.

It was nearly one o'clock on the morning of the fifth of May 1741, that Elizabeth's cries were replaced by a new sound; that of a baby's first cry. Then the house fell silent. After another quarter of an hour, Susanna came down and told Isaac that he could come up to the bedroom. He lit a candlestick from the hearth and quickly climbed the stairs to the bedroom. This was lit by about half a dozen candles and Isaac could see Elizabeth in the bed, half lying and half sitting, propped up by the pillows. In her arms she held a tiny bundle, wrapped in a linen shawl.

"Congratulations, Isaac," said Susanna, "You have a lovely baby daughter." Isaac moved to the side of the bed and sat on it next to his wife, looking down at the face of the new addition to their family. Charity, who had spent time cleaning and tidying the room, finished her work, gathered up her bag, and made to leave.

"I'll be going now, but I'll call in again later tomorrow and make sure all is well," she said. Susanna went down the stairs with her, leaving Isaac and Elizabeth together with their daughter. Isaac removed his footwear and lay fully on the bed and it was not long before the pair had drifted off into sleep.

Less than a fortnight later, the families and their friends gathered after morning service in St Margaret's Church for the baptism of Isaac and Elizabeth's daughter, whom they named Susanna, after her grandmother.

*   *   *   *   *

Tuesday the eighth of September, 1741, witnessed an event that was to have a profound effect on the town and inhabitants of King's Lynn. Isaac, Nicholas, Matthew and Stephen were at their work in the sail loft. It was just after mid-day. It had been a miserable day outside and had been raining for most of the morning, but then the wind rose to a violence that none of them had ever known before. They went to the windows and looked out, but they could hardly see across the courtyard. The noise was tremendous and the whole building seemed to be shaking. It was hard to tell from which way the wind was blowing; it seemed to batter the walls on all sides. Nicholas called to Isaac to help him and they went into the storeroom. Against the far wall, ready in case of flooding, was a pile of sacks filled with sand. Between them they dragged them across the bottom of the doorway, hoping to protect their stock of canvas and rope. Then they returned to the main loft. Mathew and Stephen had moved away from the windows and were sitting at their benches. Isaac looked at them and could see the fear in their eyes; this was something that they had not even imagined, let alone experienced in their young lives.

Isaac rejoined Nicholas by one of the windows. They could just make out in all the noise and confusion the sound of falling masonry and could make out various pieces of wood and other debris being thrown about the courtyard by the whirling wind. As they watched through the window, a tidal wave came from the direction of the river, flooding the courtyard. Then they heard a really loud crash, drowning out even the howling of the wind and seeming to last for minutes, although, in reality, it was probably not more than half a minute.

All of them now felt real fear. This part of the world was well used to storms, but this was beyond anything that any of them had known. It felt like the end of the world. The storm raged at its full intensity for around an hour, before the wind abated. When it seemed that the weather had returned to normal, they could contain their curiosity no longer. What had caused that terrible crash?

Putting on cloaks over their working clothes, they left the loft and hurried out towards Lath Street. There they found that crowds of people were on the street, all moving towards the church. They joined the throng and ran along the street. When they arrived at St Margaret's Church, they were greeted with a sight that truly astounded them. The spire, that had risen skyward from the right hand tower, was no longer there. It had disappeared, along with a section of the tower itself. Most of the crowd were now standing at the front of the church and looking in through the doors. The four sail-makers moved forwards and, with some difficulty, forced their way through to the doors. Then they saw that the remnants of the steeple were lying, shattered to pieces, across the nave of the church. Looking up they could see that the roof of the church was virtually destroyed. The lantern tower, that had stood, acting as a beacon for shipping, at the eastern end of the roof, was hanging at a precarious angle into the gaping hole.

The four moved away, hardly able to believe what had happened. Then another bystander informed everyone around him that a similar thing had happened at St Nicholas' Chapel; the spire there had also been brought down by the storm. Fortunately, it had missed the chapel itself and fallen in the church yard.

"Aye," the informant dryly commented, "it dug its own grave."

Isaac's thoughts now turned to Elizabeth and young Susanna. Were they safe? He hoped that Elizabeth hadn't chosen today to visit the Tuesday Market. He quickly explained his fears to Nicholas, who urged him to go home at once and see that all was well. Isaac needed no second bidding and hurried away along to the cottages, having to force his way against the tide of people still heading into the churchyard. He turned into Priory Lane, which had been flooded by the tidal wave. He strode through the water until he came to the cottage. Inside, the floor was awash with muddy water, but, to his immense relief, he saw Elizabeth sitting there, holding their young daughter close. Elizabeth seemed in a state of shock, unable to comprehend what had happened that day, but, when Isaac put his arms around her, she began to regain some of her composure. With the downstairs room in such a state from the flooding, Isaac persuaded her to go up to the bedroom and lay down. The clean-up could wait until after the water subsided. Isaac stayed with her for the rest of the afternoon.

*   *   *   *   *

In the weeks and months that followed, all the talk in the taverns and elsewhere was of the Great Storm. People coming from the countryside to the market brought tales of the destruction elsewhere. At least two large barns had been completely destroyed and everywhere trees had been uprooted and felled. There were also reports that Middleton Hall, a few miles out of town on the Norwich Road, had been severely damaged, with the collapse of a gable end, the destruction of several chimneys, and a weather vane being toppled from the roof.

It was also said that the Mayor and Corporation of the town had personally delivered a petition to the local Member of Parliament, Sir Robert Walpole, who was also the King's Prime Minister at the time, asking for support in raising funds to repair the two churches.

In the meantime, every able bodied man, including Isaac, gave of his free time to start the work of breaking up and clearing the broken masonry from the body of St Margaret's Church. The main part of the church could not be used yet for services, due to absence of a roof, and all worship was confined to the chancel at the eastern end of the church. The broken lantern tower was dismantled, as it was most likely to fall in its present condition. Despite protests from seafarers, who had found it to be a useful guide, it was never to be replaced. Eventually, over the next six years, the roof and interior of the church was fully repaired, but the repaired tower outside was never again adorned by a steeple.

*　　*　　*　　*　　*

At that time, England still used the Julian Calendar and the change of the year did not occur until March. So it was still 1741 the following February, when Nicholas got married. He had told his family and friends a few months before about his engagement to a girl he had met through the Friends, one Mary Hopkins. They were all invited to the wedding in early February, at the Friends' Meeting House in Cross Yard, near Lady Bridge, where the town bordered South Lynn. Before the day of the wedding, Nicholas had spoken to his family and to Isaac about the ceremony. He warned them to expect something quite different to the weddings with which they were familiar. Just how different they were about to find out.

On the day of the wedding, most of the guests, including Isaac and Elizabeth, had already taken their places in the main room of the meeting house. This was unlike any church that Isaac had known, being basically a large room, furnished with a few rows of benches and another row of benches facing them. There was also a table to one side, with a large parchment on it, together with quill pens and ink. This was the wedding certificate.

Isaac and Elizabeth had been asked by Nicholas to sit on the front row of benches, leaving a space in the middle of the row. Looking round the room, Isaac could see that there were about two dozen other people in the congregation.

The next to enter were senior members of the Friends, who would act as wedding overseers. They took their place on the benches facing the body of the room. Then came the Elstobbs; William, Margaret and William junior, and they sat on the front row of benches in the main congregation, in the space left clear by Isaac. Finally, Nicholas and his bride-to-be, Mary, entered together and sat with the overseers on the benches at the front, facing the meeting. Isaac expected that someone would lead the ceremony, rather like the vicar had done at his wedding, but instead there followed a period of silence, as everyone in the meeting seemed lost in their own thoughts. This continued for several minutes.

Eventually, Nicholas and Mary rose together and started to make their declarations, with Nicholas being the first to speak.

"In the presence fear of the Lord and in the presence of this assembly, Friends, I take this my friend, Mary Hopkins, to be my wife, promising, through divine assistance, to be unto her a loving and faithful husband, so long as we both on earth shall live."

In her turn, Mary made an identical declaration, before they both moved across and signed the wedding certificate. Then they returned to their seats, whilst one of the overseers read the certificate aloud to the meeting. Another period of silence followed…

After a few minutes, a member of the meeting stood up and gave his thoughts on the nature of marriage. More silence, as the meeting contemplated his words.

This pattern was followed for some time, with members of the congregation being moved to stand and share their feelings, sometimes with generalised statements about marriage, but more often with words of praise or good wishes for the married couple. Isaac could see that Nicholas was trying to signal to his father to stand up and say something, but William did not seem to notice. Isaac, who was sitting alongside William, nudged him and in a whispered aside, drew his attention to Nicholas. At last William realised what was wanted and stood up.

"Nicholas has been a good son to me and my wife, Margaret, and I think he has made a wise choice in Mary. We wish them both well in their marriage and hope that they will have a happy and fruitful life together." William sat down and Isaac noticed that Nicholas now was smiling. William may not share his beliefs, but he had publically received his blessing. Once more the meeting adopted a thoughtful silence.

The end of the ceremony was signaled by two of the overseers standing and shaking hands. At this point, Nicholas and Mary stood and walked together out of the meeting as man and wife. Then the rest of the congregation was asked to witness the marriage by each signing the certificate. Isaac now realised why the parchment was so large; there had to be room for all those signatures.

After the signing of the certificate, everyone filed out to an outer room, where a small meal of bread and various meats, plus some small beer to drink, was waiting. Isaac moved to Nicholas to offer his congratulations, but one thing had been bothering him and he could no longer contain his curiosity.

"Tell me one thing, Nicholas," he began, "I realise that that was a completely different form of wedding from my own, for example. There was no priest to join you together in marriage and give a blessing. How then can you really be married?"

Nicholas smiled and gently replied, "It is part of our beliefs. We feel that we each have our own relationship directly with God and we do not need another person, such as a priest, to come between us and God and act on our behalf. It is God who has married us."

Isaac nodded and gave the appearance of being satisfied with the answer, but inwardly he still harboured doubts. But, as long as Nicholas and Mary were happy…

Chapter Eight: Changes

Isaac and Elizabeth's second child was born in the March of 1742, just before the New Year was celebrated on Lady Day, the 25th March. Once more it was a daughter and, although Isaac had been hoping for a boy to carry the family name forward, he tried to hide this from Elizabeth. They called the new addition to the family Sarah. Just over a year later, another child was born, once more a daughter, whom they called Judith.

The small cottage they were renting was now becoming very crowded, with all five sharing the bedroom. Whilst it was not uncommon for couples to have large families in such circumstances, Isaac was well aware that any further expansion of the family could lead to even worse overcrowding. He was ambitious enough to want to improve his status and to be able to provide more for the family. The key to this would be to start his own business, but this would take money, of which, as yet, he still did not have enough. At this point in time, it seemed a far off dream.

At the sail loft, the two young apprentices were approaching the end of their time. Mathew Fisher would be at the end of his apprenticeship in August 1744, whilst Stephen Magnus would be time-served the following

September. Isaac could see that Nicholas would not be able to pay all three of them full wages and, in their conversations, was already beginning to question Isaac about his plans. For his part, Isaac continued to forge relationships with people who might be of help to him, particularly among the ship builders, ships' masters and merchants. It was one of the latter who was eventually to come to his aid.

The governance of King's Lynn was in the hands of the rich merchant families, who had made their fortunes with the trade through the port. These families included such names as Bagge, Browne, Hogge and Allen. Time and again, these names had appeared as Mayors, Aldermen and Councillors of the town. Stephen Allen was a wine merchant and also owned much property in the town and the surrounding countryside. Isaac had met him when supplying sails to the ships he used to import wine, mainly from Portugal, and had found him to be quite a pleasant man. Like many of the merchant class, he felt that it was in the interest of everyone to encourage trades at all levels of society and to look after the population generally. He was a councillor on the Corporation of the town and took an interest in all those with whom he had dealings.

In the summer of 1745, in a conversation at the quayside, Isaac had mentioned his ambition to set up his own sail loft and found Stephen Allen to be quite encouraging.

"That sounds like a splendid idea. The trade in the port is on the increase and we will need more ships to be built," he had said, "What is stopping you from this enterprise?"

Isaac explained about the problems of finding suitable premises, his desire for a bigger dwelling, and the main problem of finding enough money.

Stephen Allen laughed and replied that he could help with all of these matters.

"I happen to own some property near you called Hampton Court. Most of it is now divided up into tenements, but there is also quite a large warehouse attached."

Isaac knew of Hampton Court, as it was only a few yards away from where he now lived, on the other side of Lath Street. He had often looked in through the archway on Lath Street and seen the cobbled courtyard surrounded by the various tenements. He also knew that between this courtyard and the river was indeed a large warehouse. The buildings were quite old, with the earliest parts dating back to the fourteenth century. Even the latest part, on the north side of the court was about a hundred years old. It was here that John Hampton, a baker, had plied his trade in the middle of the seventeenth century, and the area had been commonly known by his name ever since. Isaac's thoughts on Hampton Court were interrupted as the councillor continued.

"There is room on the upper floor of the warehouse to set up your sail loft, with storage room below for your canvas and other materials. I mainly use the cellars for my wine, so there is plenty of room. I also have a tenement available. It is quite large and would suit a growing family."

"This is very much of interest," replied Isaac, "but what would it cost?"

"The loft and storage space would be sixteen pounds a year and the tenement four. Twenty pounds paid as five pounds on each Quarter Day."

Isaac's heart sank. This was a wonderful opportunity, but he could not see how he was to afford it.

"I have enough money to start the business and have already purchased the necessary tools and some stock of materials, but until I start earning income, I fail to see how I could afford the rent."

Once more Stephen Allen gave a small laugh.

"Don't worry, Isaac. I can help there as well. The Corporation has access to funds for just such purposes and, as a councillor, I can help you to get a loan. Various wealthy men have set up funds, which we manage. I could help you apply for, say, a loan of twenty pounds over ten years. At the end of this time, you will need to pay back a sum of twenty-five pounds. In ten years you'll probably be a very successful sail-maker, with no problem in finding such a sum."

Isaac was certainly interested in this idea, as it would certainly solve his immediate problems.

"How do I set about obtaining such a loan?" he asked.

"You will need to enlist the help of three friends, who are tradesmen in their own right and are willing to stand surety for the loan. If you default on the loan and the Corporation has to pursue you and your sureties, the penalty would be that you, or they, would have to pay fifty pounds. Do you think you can find three such friends?"

"I think so. What then?"

"Just come and see me and I will do the rest. Perhaps you would like to see the premises I have on offer. Why don't we meet again tomorrow at Hampton Court at around noon, and I will show you round?"

Isaac readily agreed. He couldn't wait for the day's work to end, so he could share all this with Elizabeth.

*   *   *   *   *

Elizabeth was indeed excited and enthusiastic about the prospect of moving to Hampton Court and of Isaac becoming his own master. Isaac set out for work the next morning with a spring in his step. When he arrived at the sail loft, he confided his plan to Nicholas, who thought it was an excellent idea. He agreed that Isaac should leave early for his lunch break and take as much time as he needed to conclude the deal.

Prompt at just before noon, Isaac arrived at Hampton Court, where he found Stephen Allen waiting. They first went round the corner into St. Margaret's Lane. They walked down the lane towards the river, with

Hampton Court on the left and the old Hanseatic warehouses on the right. Stephen Allen's warehouse was further down on the left, adjoining Hampton Court. Inside, Isaac was led up to the upper floor to see the room there. This was a long narrow room, with a few windows down one side to give light. It was nearly empty, with only a few sacks of grain stored at one end. The merchant assured him that these would be moved to the ground floor. Whilst the room was probably not wide enough to accommodate a large mainsail being laid out in its entirety, Isaac could see that most other sails would fit easily. He could always make up the larger sails in two halves and then join them, so he knew that this space would make an excellent sail loft. There was even room to store some of his canvas and rope here. He was also pleased to see that there were a pair of doors in the side wall, through which goods could be lowered to the lane below.

Isaac turned to Stephen Allen and said, "This is fine. I'm sure that this will do for my new enterprise."

"Good. Now I'll show you the tenement."

They left the warehouse and made their way back along the lane to Lath Street, before turning into the courtyard. Isaac was led across the courtyard to a door at the far end and shown inside. This led into a small room with a staircase in the corner. To the right was another door that led to a larger room with an open fireplace set into the wall that backed onto St. Margaret's Lane. There was also an oven there and Stephen Allen explained that this was probably one of the ovens that the baker, John Hampton, had used for his trade a hundred years previously. This room also had a pantry cupboard in one corner and there was a sink supplied with mains water.

The upstairs part of the tenement was again split into two rooms, one slightly larger than the other. Overall, the tenement would give them about twice as much space as their current cottage and Isaac felt quite excited about the prospect of moving here.

Isaac was also taken out of the back of the property, which was basically open land leading towards the river. He noticed that the walls of the court buildings had five vaulted arches built into the brickwork and commented on this to Stephen Allen.

"Ah, yes. At one time these were warehouses and there was a cutting leading from the river, that came right up to the building. It was big enough for small ships to unload their wares directly into the warehouses through the arches. Much of the land between here and the river was formed when small inlets like this silted up. Many of the riverside warehouses are built on the new land that formed when this happened. Once these buildings here were of less use as warehouses, they were converted to tenements and the archways were bricked up."

The two men went back through the building and into the courtyard. Isaac turned to the merchant and offered his hand.

"This will do fine and I will accept your offer. I will find the three sureties for the loan and will come back to you soon. But, one way or another, I'm going ahead. Thank you for all your help."

Stephen Allen took the proffered hand and shook it firmly.

"Well done, Isaac. I'm sure you'll not regret it."

Their business concluded, Isaac crossed the street and went down the alleyway to the cottage to tell Elizabeth the news, before returning to share it with Nicholas at the sail loft.

*   *   *   *   *

Isaac's next task was to find his three sureties. He knew where to start. Through his work, he had made contacts with many along the shoreline; in the ship-builders, local boatmen and the like. He had also met and become friends with them socially, so he set off one evening to his old haunt, the *Eight Bells*. He knew that Thomas Bonner was unlikely to be acceptable as a surety, not being a freeman of the town, nor yet in business for himself, but he knew that he was likely to find others there who would be suitable. He was pleased to see one of the people he had in mind, Thomas Taylor. Thomas was a carpenter working at a shipyard close to the South Gate of the town. As a well-established tradesman and a master of his craft, he was firmly positioned in the middle class of the population and would be acceptable as a surety.

Isaac ordered a pitcher of ale and sat down with Thomas. He explained his mission and, even before the ale had been served, Thomas agreed to act as surety. He had known Isaac for some time and knew he was to be trusted not to default on the loan.

Thomas then pointed out another old friend and acquaintance, who was in the tavern that evening. This was George Holgate. Like his father before him, George was a pilot on the river. His job was to row out to ships approaching the port and then guide them through the numerous shallows and sand banks, to reach a safe berth. This was vital at that time, as the river bed underwent many changes, sometimes through the actions of high tides, sometimes following storms. Following the great storm of 1741, for example, it had been necessary to take measures to keep the port open. This had resulted in two piers being built, one on each side of the river, where the land was being worn away and the river was in danger of silting up completely. George and his fellow pilots had to be aware of all the changes happening in the river, so they could bring the ships safely into port.

George was invited to join Isaac and Thomas and share the ale. Once again Isaac explained how he was soon to set up in business for himself and needed the loan to ensure a good start. Once again he was rewarded by an immediate agreement. There being no other likely candidates in the tavern that evening, the trio continued to sup ale and talk about the state of the town in general until fairly late in the evening. Eventually, satisfied with the progress made that evening, Isaac made his way back to the cottage and his bed.

The next day, he was able to complete the tally of sureties, when he delivered a sail to a ship on the quayside and persuaded its master, Richard Sands, to add his name to the agreement. Without wasting any further time, he sought out Stephen Allen to tell him the news and, a few days later, the councillor asked Isaac to come along to the Guildhall and sign the indenture agreeing to the loan. Over the next few days, the other signatures of the sureties were collected and the document was ready to be presented to the Corporation.

Now that his finances were sorted out and knowing that he would have the money to pay his rent to Stephen Allen at the next Quarter Day, Isaac made the move to Hampton Court in October. The benches, tools and material he had spent so much time acquiring were transported to the new sail loft, with the help of Nicholas, Mathew and Stephen, who also lent a hand moving his furniture from the cottage to the Hampton Court tenement. Once again, Isaac felt the excitement of a new chapter opening up in his life.

Chapter Nine: Alarms, Tragedy and Democracy.

Isaac had set up his business and taken on a number of commissions. At this point, he was working alone, not feeling ready yet to take on the responsibility of having extra staff. Until he had earned enough from this early work, he would not be able to pay a skilled sail-maker, whilst he needed to establish a reputation before he would be asked to take on an apprentice.

During the months of September, October and November, there had been much talk in the town, particularly in the taverns, about the activities of Charles Stuart, the Young Pretender, who had landed in Scotland in early September and set about raising an army to march south and claim the throne. They had had an early success against a force under General Cope, whom they defeated at Prestonpans, near Edinburgh, on the 21st September.

In late October, having gathered an army of around eight thousand men, the rebels moved south. Moving against them was an army led by the Duke of Cumberland. It had appeared that they would be likely to meet in battle on the Cheshire Plain, but then Charles Stuart changed direction, veering to the east and marched on Derby.

When this news reached King's Lynn, it caused a general panic. Few of the local population had any real idea of the geography of England and imagined that the town was in the line of the rebels' march on the capital. Some talked of stories they had heard about when the town was besieged during the Civil War in 1643. Then it had been forced to capitulate to the Parliamentarian forces and many were worried that the current defences would not be able to resist the Young Pretender and his Highland rebels. As a result, many an able-bodied man, including Isaac, hurried to the area outside the South Gate, which was considered the most logical approach to the town, where they proceeded to build an earthwork, as an additional line of defence in front of the town walls. The workers were led in this enterprise by the Mayor, Philip Case, and the entire Corporation. Isaac saw his new landlord, Stephen Allen, working hard with pick-axe and shovel, to help build this new defence.

Whether the earthwork would have been very effective is open to some doubt. The men had completed one section of it and were resting on their shovels, admiring their handiwork, when a greyhound, that one of them had brought along, broke loose from the group and ran easily over the top of the mound of soil and other debris, before returning, obviously pleased with his adventure. This took the wind out of the sails of some of those present.

"If a dog can get over it so easily, what's to stop those Highlanders?" was the comment from one exhausted worker. As it happened, this was never to be put to the test, as the rebel army retreated back towards Scotland, followed by the Duke of Cumberland. There were further alarms in the town, particularly when two travelling Scotsmen were apprehended in the Marshland area, west of the river. Suspected of being rebel spies, they were arrested and brought to King's Lynn for questioning. The story that was being told in the taverns was that when they were asked if they had any arms, they replied, "Yes, two!" holding their hands aloft. Eventually came the news that Charles Stuart and his army had been beaten at the battle of Culloden and the town could return to normal, after all the excitement.

*　　*　　*　　*　　*

The winter of 1745 was quite severe and there was a lot of sickness amongst the population of King's Lynn. Among the major scourges of the general population were such diseases as smallpox and typhoid fever. The latter, usually simply known as "the fever", was contracted mainly from polluted water and was very common in the poorer parts of the town.

Smallpox was a horrible disease, producing a rash all over the body, which later became fluid filled blisters. About four in ten victims died of the disease and if a person did survive, they would often be scarred for life and in some cases left blind. Naturally, this disease was feared by all and the only preventative recourse was a process called variolation, which many parents adopted for their children. The subject of variolation would be given a mild form of the disease, in the hope that they would build up immunity. The general method would be to make a powder from ground scabs from a victim of a minor form of the disease and then rub these into a puncture or scratch in the skin, usually on the hand. The result would be that the person inoculated in this manner would develop symptoms similar to smallpox, but, if they were in good health otherwise, they would soon recover and would then be immune to the disease. Isaac and Elizabeth had had their children inoculated in this way.

Isaac was fearful for the health of his children, particularly the two younger ones. It was common for up to half the children to succumb to one disease or another before the age of five. Isaac had a good supply of coal and was able to keep the tenement reasonably warm. The children rarely left the house at this time of the year. Nevertheless, during the last week of January, Susanna became ill. She complained of a headache and other aches in her joints, finding it hard to lay on her back in comfort. Just by feeling her forehead, it was easy to tell she was running a fever. Elizabeth tried to feed her some broth, but this only provoked vomiting, which became quite violent at times.

Isaac needed help and advice, so he did what most people of his class would do; he went to an apothecary who had premises on the High Street. The services of a physician, with their sword at their side and their silver topped cane denoting their genteel status, would be out of his financial reach. The apothecary listened to Isaac's description of Susanna's symptoms and then made up a potion, which was basically an opiate. Isaac paid him the florin requested and hurried home with this precious bottle.

Elizabeth managed to get Susanna to take a few drops of the potion, which seemed to offer some relief. Susanna did not complain so much about the pains and spent most of the time sleeping. Indeed, for several days there appeared to be an improvement in her condition. Isaac and Elizabeth had every hope that she would make a full recovery. After work each day, Isaac would hurry home to see how his daughter fared.

Then he would go out again and cross over to St. Margaret's church. The roof destroyed in the great storm was still under repair, so he would make his way to the east end of the church and go into the chancel to pray for his daughter's recovery.

In spite of these signs of improvement, some two weeks after the onset of the illness, she suddenly took a turn for the worse. She developed a chesty cough and had great difficulty breathing, often gasping for air. Her fever, which had been receding, was now worse than ever. She could hardly bear to have the bed sheets covering her and was constantly in a sweat. The apothecary's potion now had little effect. In spite of all of Elizabeth's tender care, or the prayers offered up by Isaac in St. Margaret's, Susanna died in the second week of February. Isaac's next visit to the church was to make the arrangements for her funeral, which took place on the seventeenth of the month, leaving Isaac and Elizabeth to mourn the loss of their firstborn child.

*   *   *   *   *

After Susanna's death, Isaac and Elizabeth received much sympathy and support from friends and family. With the high rate of infant mortality, virtually everyone they knew had had a similar experience at some time. One person who could certainly feel their grief more than most was Nicholas. His wife, Mary had given birth to a daughter almost exactly a year after their wedding, but the child, also called Mary, had died within a month. Isaac had naturally sympathised with him then and tried to support him. Now it was Nicholas's turn to offer support.

Isaac and Elizabeth coped with the loss in their individual ways. Elizabeth became even more protective of her other daughters and spent a lot of time with one or the other in her arms, as she sat quietly in front of the fire. Isaac, meantime, threw himself into his work. He would be at the sail loft at first light and would work through the day, with only brief breaks to eat, sometimes finishing well after sunset, working by the light of oil lamps. His industry was rewarded by the fact that his reputation grew as being a hard and conscientious worker, and the orders came in a steady flow. At times he had so much work in hand that he found it hard to cope with it all. It was fortuitous, therefore, when, one day in early spring, he received a visitor at the loft.

The man who stood before him was familiar to Isaac, although he looked very gaunt and appeared much older than his years. It was Daniel Locust, a sail-maker, who was, in fact, only about six years older than Isaac. Isaac had known him from when he had been first apprenticed to William Elstobb in May 1729. Daniel was then in his last year of his own apprenticeship. He had worked for a time for William, but had then decided to go to sea, perhaps inspired by William's tales of his time on board ship. He had served with the Royal Navy as a sail-maker for a dozen years and had recently returned to King's Lynn, looking to settle down ashore. He had heard that Isaac was now in business on his own and hoped that there would be a place for an experienced sail-maker.

Somewhat shocked at his appearance, Isaac quizzed him on his experiences in the navy. It transpired that he had sailed over much of the world, particularly on his last voyage. He had been a sailor on board *HMS Centurion* during Commodore Anson's ill-fated expedition to attack Spanish possessions in the Pacific. Daniel was reluctant to talk much about his experience, but did say that, out of the nearly two thousand men that were aboard the ships of the original squadron of six warships and two merchant vessels, only five hundred survived. The *Centurion* suffered particularly badly, with scarcely one in ten left alive. Many had died of scurvy and Daniel himself had suffered with this affliction, which accounted for his current appearance and the fact that he had been allowed to leave the service on the Centurion's eventual return to England. The war against Spain, known as the War of Jenkin's Ear and conducted mainly in the New World, was still ongoing, although there had been few major clashes between the two powers since 1742 and it was now overshadowed by events in mainland Europe.

Daniel's main work on board ship had been in the repairing of sails damaged in storms or in battle and he confessed that he had had little chance to make new sails. Isaac knew he would have had a good grounding during his service with William Elstobb and he was also coming to realise that he couldn't continue much longer without some assistance, as the long hours were beginning to take their toll.

"Fine," he said at last, "I'm prepared to give you a chance, if you can show me that your skills are still up to the job. Sit down here and continue this seam."

At that, Isaac rose from his seat at the bench and motioned Daniel to take his place. Then he handed over the sail which he had been sewing.

"I'm just going to do some paperwork. Show me a good job and we'll talk terms." Isaac went over to the desk he had in the corner of the room and busied himself there for about half an hour, whilst Daniel continued sewing the seam. When Isaac returned, he saw that Daniel had made good progress. The seam itself was neatly sewn and straight. Isaac was satisfied.

A short discussion followed. To Isaac's surprise, Daniel was happy to accept a lower wage than normal, with the promise of more if the business prospered. Up to this point, Daniel had only spoken of the hardships suffered during the time spent on the *Centurion*, but had not mentioned the one high spot of the expedition, when the Spanish treasure galleon, the *Neustra Señora de Covadonga*, had been captured. Isaac had heard of this, but did not appreciate the prize money that Daniel would have earned from this victory. Even as an ordinary seaman, he would have pocketed around three hundred pounds. The two men settled on twenty-five pounds a year and Isaac now had an extra pair of hands to share the load.

*   *   *   *   *

In the summer of 1747, a General Election was called with barely three weeks notice and this was to bring great excitement to King's Lynn. The borough returned two burgesses to serve as Members of Parliament and it was quite usual for there to be only two candidates, who were thus returned unopposed. It appeared that this would be the case this time as, up until a week before the election, there were only two declared candidates, Sir John Turner and Horatio Walpole.

Horatio Walpole was the nephew of the great Sir Robert Walpole, who had been Prime Minister under both George I and George II. Sir Robert had resigned in 1742 and had been made a peer, the Earl of Orford. He had died in 1745 and his son, also named Robert, had succeeded to the title. This latter Robert Walpole was also High Steward of Lynn.

Sir John Turner came from a prominent King's Lynn family, that had been active in local affairs for nearly a century, having provided its Mayor on nine occasions to date, and four Turners, including Sir John, had sat as Members of Parliament.. It had been a previous Sir John who, in 1683, had commissioned the building of the town's Custom House by Henry Bell, who was also responsible for the *Dike's Head*. However, the family were not that popular, as many felt that, when some of them had held the position of Commissioner of the Treasury and other posts concerned with the town's finances and trade, they had abused those positions to make money for themselves and this was how they had risen to be amongst the richest men in the town.

Some of the supporters of Sir John were worried that another candidate might materialise and approached the High Steward to express their concerns. He had tried to reassure them by showing them a letter he had received from the possible candidate, William Folkes, pledging that he would not intervene. However, he was to prove unreliable in this respect, as he declared his intention to stand a little more than a week before the election. Immediately the town was in a state of turmoil, as people began to take sides. Although freemen of the town were the only ones with a vote, everyone seemed to have an opinion and set about persuading those with a vote to come round to their way of thinking. Most of the discussion took place in the taverns of the town and, at times, it seemed that the whole populace were in a state of inebriation, as arguments raged back and forth. Often, these arguments would flare up into something more violent and drunken brawls between rival factions were commonplace.

William Folkes was a lawyer with a London practice and was now travelling to King's Lynn to begin his campaign. His main backers in the town started the campaign for him by making sure that the taverns where his supporters met were serving free ale on his account. The backers of Mr Walpole and Sir John Turner did exactly the same in their supporters' taverns. Quite naturally, most of the population, men, women and even children, took liberal advantage of this largesse.

The Walpole supporters were certain in their own minds that their man would prevail. After all, a Walpole had represented King's Lynn in Parliament since the Restoration of King Charles II in 1660. Their triumphant song could often be heard in the taverns they frequented.

> *Come fill up a bumper, and round let us stand;*
> *Old England's our toast, take your glasses in hand –*
> *May loyalty, liberty, flourish in Lynn,*
> *And a Walpole, a Walpole, for ever be in.*
> *Hearts of oak are we still and true honest men,*
> *We always are ready,*
> *Steady, boys, steady,*
> *And a Walpole, a Walpole, shall ever be in!*

Their confidence was probably not misplaced and the real contest would be between Sir John and William Folkes.

Folkes was the first to appear in person, as Walpole and Turner, believing that there would not be a contest, were elsewhere in the country. Horatio Walpole had simply sent a letter explaining his views on the election and hoped that this would suffice, whilst Sir John was at one of his estates in Gloucestershire, where his wife was expected to give birth at any time. When William Folkes arrived at King's Lynn, the procession accompanying him was a sight to behold. There were dozens of supporters on horseback, drummers, men waving flags and banners, and others discharging muskets into the air. This all made a tremendous noise, bringing out a large crowd to see what was happening. Folkes had chosen blue as his campaign colour and his supporters showed their allegiance by wearing something of that colour. Whilst the women could find a blue dress and some of the men had jackets of that colour, many of the men were happy just to pin a blue cockade to their hat. The procession made its way to the Tuesday Market Place, where Folkes made a speech from the balcony of the Market Cross. His main points were aimed at Sir John and he succeeded in bringing his drunken supporters to a state of frenzy.

Amongst the crowd was Isaac, who had left his bench in the sail loft, to determine the cause of the commotion. His work had kept him busy of late and he had not been taking advantage of the free ale. As yet, he was not sure where his sympathies would lie on election day, the following Monday. Whilst he had heard a lot about the Walpoles, he had not personally encountered any of the family, neither had he any real love for the Turners. But he knew that he was likely to be approached for his vote, as a freeman of the town. He had not yet had a chance to cast a vote since gaining that status, as previous elections had been uncontested. He listened to the speech with interest, before returning to his work.

Later that day, Isaac had a visitor. It was Nicholas Elstobb. Isaac was shocked at his appearance. He had not seen his old friend and former employer for some months, but he had heard reports about Nicholas suffering from ill health. His features certainly confirmed this. His face looked drawn and much thinner than previously. His eyes were sunken and he had an ashen complexion. Beads of sweat stood out on his forehead and he had a cough that seemed to rattle in his throat. Isaac noticed that the handkerchief he held in front of his mouth when trying to control the coughing was stained with blood. From time to time he would take a sip from a small bottle, which Isaac recognised as being of a type supplied by the apothecary and guessed, quite accurately, that it contained an opiate. Nicholas was not a well man and when he spoke his voice was weaker than normal.

"Did you hear the speech today?"

"Indeed I did," replied Isaac.

"Folkes could be the man to give the Turners a bloody nose. There's a meeting at the *Dog* tonight of those who would see this happen. Will you come?"

Isaac considered for a moment and decided he had little to lose by acceding to his friend's request.

"Yes, I will. At what time will it start?"

"Around seven o'clock. I'm pleased you will come and I'll see you there later."

At that, Nicholas left. Isaac could hear him coughing and wheezing as he descended the stairs from the sail loft and left the building. What he had seen and heard made him very worried for Nicholas. He had seen similar cases before and the outcome had not been good.

Having briefly been home for his evening meal, Isaac was later to be found at the *Dog* tavern, along with his employee, Daniel Locust. The tavern was full to overflowing, with many supporters of William Folkes enjoying his hospitality. Isaac and Daniel, however, were directed to a back room, where a number of others were gathered. These were those with a vote, the freemen of the town that Folkes wanted to win over. Looking around, Isaac recognised quite a few of those in the room. Many were merchants and tradesmen that he had dealings with, including his landlord, Stephen Allen, and his son, also called Stephen. He also saw Nicholas, a tankard of ale in hand, talking with a man that Isaac recognised as John Harvey, the apothecary he had consulted during Susanna's fatal illness. Isaac moved across to join them and greeted Nicholas.

"Nicholas, good evening. Here I am, as promised. Are your father and brother here tonight?"

"I'm afraid not," came the reply, "They are for Sir John Turner and I cannot persuade them otherwise. I think my brother has an eye on obtaining employment from the council and Turner has a lot of influence there. He has managed to persuade my father that he should support him in this."

As they conversed further, Isaac commented on the fact that Nicholas was enjoying the ale being freely supplied.

"I thought the Quakers were not in favour of strong drink, Nicholas," he said, a little mischievously.

"True," his friend replied, "but I find that it is one of the few things that help me to keep the pain from my chest tolerable. It's cheaper than the mixture I get from John here. I'm sure I should be permitted one vice in this life."

The men continued to talk together for a few minutes, until a buzz of excitement in the room, followed by enthusiastic applause, signalled the arrival of the candidate.

William Folkes, as an attorney, was well used to public speaking and launched into a well-prepared speech. He thanked all for their support and for coming to the meeting tonight. He pointed out the faults that he found in his main opponent, Sir John Turner, and hinted at the suspicion that he had been feathering his own nest at the expense of the town's Treasury. He promised all those that gave him their vote that they would be remembered and rewarded later. Finally, he urged them to talk to other freemen of the town and to try to persuade them to come over to his side. He finished to another burst of boisterous applause and many toasts to his health, made with the ale he himself had provided. Then one of his main supporters, the parson and schoolteacher, John Money, advised everyone that they would stand the best chance of seeing their man elected if they "plumped" for him; that is to say, not to use both the votes they had, but to cast a single vote in favour of Folkes.

The evening continued with more ale and a fine spread of food, again paid for by the candidate. Isaac used the time to move around and talk with several of the merchants that he knew had at least part ownership of a ship, in the hope that this might bring him his future reward in the form of more business.

As Isaac left the tavern later in the evening, he found that he was following Stephen Allen and his son out of the door. They were heading towards their carriage, waiting in the street outside, when a group of Turner supporters, wearing red scarves to denote their allegiance, came along the street. These were obviously under the influence of drink and equally obviously looking for trouble, as they carried an assortment of wooden clubs and billysticks with them. Seeing Stephen Allen approaching his carriage, a cry went up and they ran towards him. Isaac, Daniel and a number of others moved to intercept them. The first of the Turner supporters had almost reached the merchant and raised his stick to strike him. Reaching out, Isaac managed to grab the shaft of the stick and wrestle it from the man's grasp. He quickly swung the stick round and delivered a blow to the man's midriff, causing him to double up and lose his balance. This show of defiance on Isaac's part seemed to deter the rest of the Turner men and they stopped their advance. Quickly, Stephen Allen and his son were ushered into their carriage and departed the scene. By now, more men had emerged from the *Dog* and the blues now greatly outnumbered the reds, who now decided that, having lost their main target, they would get no satisfaction here and retreated back along the street. After a few minutes, assured that no more troublemakers were coming their way, Isaac made his farewells and walked back to his home.

The election took place on Monday the 29th June, when the freemen of the borough went to the Tuesday Market Place to cast their votes. There had been much discussion in the Folkes' camp concerning possible violence at the election, or on the way there. After all, the King's Lynn centre of power for the Turner family was the *Duke's Head*, which stood alongside the Tuesday Market Place. Stephen Allen approached Isaac and suggested that, as someone who had already shown his mettle in dealing with Turner's thugs, he would be a good man to lead a group of the Folkes' supporters to the vote. Isaac was indeed a strong man; years of manhandling the bales of canvas had built up his strength and he was certainly capable of handling himself well. It was agreed that some of the voters would make their way from the *Dog* to the Tuesday Market Place in a group, with Isaac and others who could acquit themselves well in any trouble being well to the front of the group. These included Roger Worman, a bricklayer, Benjamin Bryan, a mariner, Stephen Allen junior, and a group of butchers, Robert Ashley, William Green, Richard Secker and William Dillingham.

The group met no trouble as they made their way along King Street to the Tuesday Market Place. A great crowd of townspeople had gathered here to witness the vote, which was taking place at the Market Cross. Most of the crowd, of course, did not have a vote, not being freemen of the town, but that didn't prevent them from making it clear which of the candidates they favoured. The square was decorated with banners of the candidates' colours; orange for Walpole, red for Turner and blue for Folkes. These colours extended to the clothing and cockades of the various supporters, so it was not hard to distinguish friend from opponent. As the group of Folkes' supporters made their way toward the Market Cross at the far side of the square, they were greeted with a barrage of advice about how to vote, some of it threatening in nature, particularly from the Turner faction, but there were also cheers from those sporting blue favours. As they got nearer to the cross, their passage was made a little easier, as the town constables and the redcoats had cleared a space in front of the voting booth. This consisted of a large raised platform, divided into four parts. Three of these were set aside for the candidates and supporting speakers, who could address the voters as they made their way to the fourth section, set between the Folkes and Turner platforms, where the poll clerks were sitting at a table, ready to record the votes in the official poll books. Each freeman approached the table and, after identifying himself as a freeman of the town by showing his certificate of freedom, he would then declare on behalf of which candidate or candidates (for he could exercise two votes) he wished to cast his votes. The clerk would record his name, place of residence, occupation and votes in the poll book. It was a slow process and Isaac's group had to endure about thirty minutes while they all voted. The voting was by no means confidential and the crowd knew exactly how they were voting, so they had to suffer a lot of verbal abuse from the Turner faction. Fortunately, it was no more than words and the crowd were kept well back from the vote itself. At last, it was Isaac's turn to vote and he cast a single vote, as agreed, for William Folkes. Once all in the group had voted, they made their way back to the *Dog*, to await news of the result.

They would not have long to wait, as voting was due to finish by early evening and it would then take a very short time to tally the few hundred votes involved. In the meantime, the tavern was crowded with so-called supporters, enjoying William Folkes' bounty, as all the ale and refreshments were still on his account. Isaac noticed that Nicholas, who had voted earlier in the day, was sitting on a bench with the apothecary, John Harvey. Both had apparently been partaking of the candidate's generosity for some time, for they were almost insensible with drink.

At about seven o'clock, a man burst into the tavern with the news for which they had all been waiting.

"The result is out and I'm afraid it's not good. Walpole 199 votes, Turner 184 and Folkes 131. Mr Folkes is on his way here now."

A groan went up from the company, followed by a rush to replenish their tankards, in case this result signalled the end of the free drink. There was much discussion about the strength of the votes and it was generally thought that the richer merchants and most members of the Corporation had used their power and influence to see Sir John elected. Comments were made about the number of people with connections to the Turner family who had been made freemen during the early part of the year and many of those voting said that they had been approached with attempts to buy their vote.

When William Folkes appeared, he thanked all those who had voted for him and then declared that, to general delight, the free ale would continue to flow that evening. He would return to London the following day, rather poorer than he arrived at the start of the campaign. Each of the candidates had spent in the region of two thousand pounds in hospitality, bribes and other expenses, during the short period before the election.

Whilst Folkes' supporters were now consoling themselves with copious amounts of ale, Turner's victorious celebration at the *Duke's Head* was crowned with a feast and an entertainment from a company of strolling players, in a production designed to mock William Folkes and his main supporters.

Isaac, mindful that he would need to be working at first light the following morning, was about to leave for home, when he noticed that Nicholas and his companion had both collapsed onto the floor. Whilst he cared little for the apothecary, he was anxious about Nicholas, in light of his obvious poor health, so he hastened to try and rouse him. He could get very little sense out of him, but did manage to drag him to his feet. He was alarmed to notice that the front of his clothing was stained in blood, which he had been bringing up during his frequent bouts of coughing. Leaving John Harvey laying on the floor, he half carried Nicholas out of the *Dog* and set out along the streets for the house where he knew Mary Elstobb would be waiting anxiously. When he arrived there, Mary confirmed that Nicholas was indeed very ill, to the point where she had had to take over most of his business affairs and the apprentices were doing nearly all the work. However, Nicholas would not be consulting John Harvey again, as the apothecary never came out of his drunken stupor and died on the floor of the *Dog*, where he was discovered the next day.

A few days later, the Folkes' supporters had one last rally for the funeral of John Harvey. They all met at the *Dog* tavern and then marched, two by two, behind the coffin of the apothecary, as it was carried on the back of a cart, on its final journey to St Margaret's, where he was laid to rest. Then the assembly moved back to the tavern, where many hours were spent toasting William Folkes and also drinking to the memory of John Harvey, now considered, rather incongruously, a martyr to the cause.

A few days after that, all the freeman of the town, together with their wives, whether they were for Sir John Turner or not, were invited to a ball at the *Duke's Head*. It would seem that Sir John had been taken aback by the opposition to him at the election and was already thinking about the next one.

Chapter Ten: Additions and Responsibilities

During all the commotion of the election, Isaac had other matters with which to attend. For many years he had known a ship's master called Henry Crow, who had a young son, also called Henry. Henry and his family now lived in another of the tenements at Hampton Court and Isaac was used to seeing the younger Henry about the place. One day, earlier that year, he had been approached by the senior Henry, who had a request.

"Isaac," began the master mariner, "I'd like my son to have a trade that would be useful to him, whether he ends up on land or sea. Would you be prepared to take him as your apprentice, when he reaches fourteen this summer?"

Isaac had been considering taking on an apprentice, now that his business was growing, and knew that Henry Crow could help him with introductions to other master mariners. He also knew that young Henry had been well educated up to this point and was a pleasant enough lad.

"I'd be glad to, Henry. There will, of course, be the usual consideration for his training." Isaac was referring to the ten guineas to be paid at the start of the apprenticeship, when the indentures were drawn up. "When do you want him to start?"

"His birthday is in May, so the beginning of June would be about right."

"Agreed." The two men shook hands and Isaac gained his first apprentice. At the same time, he wistfully wondered how long, if ever, it would be before he had a son of his own to train to succeed him.

In the months that followed, young Henry proved to be a willing worker. He was strong for his age and was able to carry the bales of canvas from the storage area to the floor of the loft. The other menial tasks about the loft, that Isaac and Daniel did not wish to do, were no problem to Henry. Isaac gave him his own bench and set of tools and he set about learning the craft. He could practise joining strips of canvas and forming seams along the edges, using the off-cuts of canvas that were left after a pattern had been cut out on the sail loft floor. He proved to be a quick learner and soon could sew quite well, although his hands often became very sore, as they had not yet been hardened by the hours, months and years that a fully-fledged sail-maker would have spent pushing the needle through the canvas with the aid of the stitching palm. He was, however, keen to succeed in learning the trade and bore this discomfort without complaint.

Henry expected to follow his father to sea at some point and was fascinated by the tales that Daniel had to tell about his time in the Royal Navy.

Over time, Daniel began to tell more about his last voyage, which had taken him around the world over a period of nearly four years. Whilst some tales would fire young Henry's imagination, such as the landing on a remote Pacific island to effect repairs, or visits to exotic ports like Canton or Macau, Daniel did not hold back in telling of the hardships they had suffered and of the men who had been lost in battle and through sickness. His descriptions of men being blown apart by enemy cannon fire were quite blood-curdling, but even more poignant were the stories of how he had watched close friends suffer and die slowly from scurvy. At one point, eight to ten men were dying every day. He himself had only survived by their reaching the island of Tinian, north-east of Guam, where they found an abundance of fresh fruit, greens, water and even cattle. Daniel claimed that he owed his life to the breadfruit, which grew there plentifully.

Even these tales of hardship did little to faze Henry. After all, if he joined his father, they would be sailing up and down the coast in a merchant ship. There would be no battles to fear, or long periods away from fresh rations. Of course, there were always dangers at sea, but Henry was either oblivious to these or dismissed them with the eternal optimism of youth; nothing like that would ever happen to him.

*   *   *   *   *

Since the move to Hampton Court, family life for Isaac and Elizabeth was greatly improved. The extra space allowed the children to sleep in a separate room and Isaac and Elizabeth could enjoy time together in each other's company. Isaac was also happy with the way that the business was going, as it continued to grow. So when Elizabeth told him in early summer that she was again expecting, Isaac was overjoyed at the news. He knew that Elizabeth had been hit hard by the death of Susanna and, for a time, there had been a bit of tension in their marriage. But now that seemed to be behind them and Isaac found himself once more hoping for the son who might one day take over from him.

As his landlord and also a very good customer, Isaac had many dealings with Stephen Allen, so he was not surprised when the merchant visited the loft in late July. However, Stephen had not come as either landlord or client, but as a representative of the Council. He was here to recruit Isaac.

"Isaac," he began, "I have always been impressed by your character and by the fact that you are prepared to stand up to defend what you believe to be right. I well remember the incident outside the *Dog*, when you saved me from a sore head, or worse."

Isaac wondered to what all this was leading, but, as was his wont, kept quiet and waited for the Councillor to get to the point.

"As you may know," continued Stephen, "each year the Leet Court of the town elects constables and headboroughs from the various wards of the town."

Isaac did indeed know of this. The Leet court was another branch of the administration of the town, but in reality was the Council itself and decisions about the appointment of these offices were made at a General Congregation of the Council. Each ward would have a constable, otherwise known as the captain of the ward, and there were also two headboroughs of the ward, who, amongst many other duties, assisted the constable in maintaining order.

"It has been suggested that you would be an excellent choice as constable for the Stonegate ward."

"I'm honoured to be considered," replied Isaac, "but I wonder how this would impact on my business. Will I have the time?"

"It's true that you will have to spend some time on your duties, but, for this ward, this mainly centres on the Saturday Market Place. You can share the night patrols with the headboroughs and, of course, there will be a disbursement from the town coffers for your trouble. Also consider how it will help you to take on a civic post. It will bring you in contact with many Aldermen and Councillors; this can only be good for your business."

The two men continued to debate the pros and cons of Isaac accepting the nomination for some time. Eventually, Isaac agreed to his name going forward for a tour of duty that would last a year. Stephen Allen left the loft a satisfied man, having achieved his purpose.

Thus it was that on the 21st of October 1748, Isaac was elected and sworn in as one of the town's ten constables, each representing a ward of King's Lynn. Also elected were two headboroughs for each ward; those for the Stonegate ward were John Mathias, a miller, and James Dale, a cooper.

The duties of the constable centred round keeping order in the town. Generally speaking this was not too onerous a task, as King's Lynn was basically a hard-working town and most of its citizens were too tired after a long day at work to do other than go home to their beds. The places where petty crime was rife were the markets, as cutpurses and pickpockets took advantage of the crowds to ply their trade. Isaac and his two helpers would need to be at the Saturday Market Place early and spend the day watching for such crime. It was convenient for them that the town gaol was just across the road in the Guildhall building.

The headboroughs were also responsible for assisting other town officials in checking the weights and scales used by the various stallholders, to see that they were measuring accurately. This could often lead to arguments, particularly from the butchers, and even threats of violence against the headborough who challenged the measures. Isaac was involved in such an instance within the first month of being constable.

A complaint had been made to John Mathias that one of the butchers was selling short measure and had gone to investigate. He had asked the butcher concerned that the weights and scales were checked against the standard weights they had for such a purpose and had received, in rather impolite language, a refusal from the man. Other butchers on nearby stalls, seeing a chance to challenge the authority of the newly appointed official, backed up the obstinate butcher and things soon descended into a general shouting match. Isaac and James Dale, hearing this, came to join their fellow official. Isaac's first thought was to isolate the butcher at the centre of the row from the others supporting him, so he went around these, pointing out that they were losing business during the confrontation, as customers were avoiding the scene of the trouble and moving to other parts of the markets. This proved to be a convincing argument and soon the three officials had only the one man with whom to deal.

Seeing that he was now just one man against three, the butcher calmed down and tried another tactic.

"Look here, I'm only trying to make a living." he said, "Sometimes I need to get the best deal I can and make sure everything is going in my favour. Just let me carry on as I am and there'll be some free meat for you all at the end of the day."

"I see," replied Isaac, tapping the palm of his hand with the billystick he was holding, "After the threats you made earlier, you're now trying to bribe us to turn a blind eye to you cheating your customers?"

The butcher's face reddened, as he tried to contain his anger and discomfort. He was a well-built man and would have perhaps resorted to violence against any one of the officials, but realised he could not take on all three, who had been chosen as much for their physical presence as for their sense of civic duty. Isaac spoke again.

"I'll give you a simple choice. Either you produce a set of scale and weights that we can check to be fair, or you'll be spending the rest of the day, or maybe longer, over the way in a cell. It's your choice. In the meantime, we will check these weights."

Clearly unhappy and cursing at his misfortune, the butcher surrendered his scales and weights. As suspected, they were not accurate. Whilst the scales were balanced correctly, the weights were shy of their marked weight by around a tenth. The base of each weight had been hollowed out and filled with clay, before being painted to disguise the fraud. The weights were confiscated and Isaac issued a warning to the butcher.

"Whatever has happened in the past, we are not going to tolerate cheating in this market. If you have a good set of weights, we will let you carry on trading. But if we ever catch you trying this trick again, I will see to it that your license to trade here, or elsewhere in the town, is revoked. And you can spread the word to your fellows that we will be similarly intolerant to anyone else we catch."

As it happened, the man had a good set of weights hidden under his stall. Obviously, he had not been quick enough today to have them in use when he was challenged by the headborough. Isaac and his two companions continued their patrol of the market, satisfied that they had managed to defuse a threatening situation and stamp their authority on the traders; at least, for now.

At least two or three times a week, Isaac, in company with other constables, would patrol the streets of King's Lynn late into the evening, until all seemed quiet. Even at night the streets were not completely dark, as there was a local ordinance that required householders to place a light outside their houses. These were oil lamps or torches made from rushes soaked in tar. The main job of the patrol was to collect any stray drunks left wandering the streets after leaving the taverns and help them on their way home. Rarely, however, would they venture inside some of the more notorious taverns, such as the Town Arms, which stood alongside the Guildhall, as the welcome they could expect would not be friendly. It was safer to wait until the inebriated men were out on the street and separated from their fellows.

Often they would find homeless vagrants, who had come into town from the countryside to seek a better life. These would be taken to the gaol and might eventually find themselves before the Guildhall court, which would usually order them to be returned to their settlement. In a way, the constables were doing all these nocturnal wanderers a favour, as, with King's Lynn being a port, press gangs were often to be found in the streets near the harbour, seeking out recruits for the navy.

The gaol-house had been situated for centuries on the ground floor of the Guildhall building. It was certainly an uninviting place to find oneself and acted as a good deterrent to the petty criminal. The cells were abot eight feet by eight feet square, furnished only with a wooden bed, a few blankets, straw, and a slop bucket. The only light in the cell was that that filtered in from two heavily barred slits, either side of the heavy metal door. Of course, while each prisoner would be in solitary confinement, he would not necessarily be alone, as rats and other vermin were ever present. All in all, not a pleasant experience.

At busy times of the year, like at the annual Mart, or other public occasions, all the constables and headboroughs would be needed to keep order in the Tuesday Market Place; the local Redcoats were really only there for appearances, being mostly very advanced in years. Taking everything together, between running his business and performing his civic duty as constable, Isaac was kept busy and, after spending two years as constable for the ward, would be quite glad when he was able to pass the responsibility on to another in late 1750.

*   *   *   *   *

Elizabeth gave birth in mid-January; another daughter. Once more, Isaac had mixed feelings. On the one hand there was joy in a safe delivery for both mother and baby, but still there was the longing for a son. Elizabeth, on the other hand, was overjoyed. She was convinced that her dead daughter had been returned to her in the form of this new life.

She insisted that they should name her new daughter Susanna and Isaac readily agreed. A short time later, on the 24th January, the christening took place in St Margaret's Church, which was now restored to much of its former glory after the repairs to the roof and nave had been completed. Despite a general levy on the townspeople, together with generous contributions from the late Sir Robert Walpole and even the king himself, it had not been possible to find the funds to replace the steeple that fell in the great storm of 1741, whilst the lantern tower on the roof had also been removed and not replaced. Even with the interior restored, Isaac still found it strange to see the church without its crowning glories.

After the christening, Isaac, Elizabeth and their daughters made their way to the *Eight Bells*, where the Bonners had laid on a small family celebration. Isaac noticed his former master, William Elstobb, among the company and was eager to have a talk with him. Isaac was pleased to see that, in spite of his seventy-seven years, the old man still was quite sprightly and seemed in good health. Isaac took him to one of the alcoves in the main tavern and began by asking for news of William and Nicholas.

"I'm afraid it is not all good news," replied William, "William is quite successful now as a surveyor and spends most of his time in Norwich. We've helped him to buy a house here in King's Lynn, But he's travelling a lot. You know he's married now, of course." Isaac had heard of this, but had yet to meet the younger William's bride.

"Well, there lies the reason for not being here today," continued the old sail-maker, "So far he and Ann, his wife, have had two daughters, but they both died within months. With the last one being buried here only a few months ago, he felt he didn't want to subject Ann to the journey and the memories it would arouse in her. He asked me to say sorry to yourself and Elizabeth."

"I understand. Will you pass on our sympathies, please. We know exactly how they are feeling. I saw Nicholas a while back and he seemed really sick. Is he better now?"

"Unfortunately, not. If anything, he's getting worse. I'm spending a bit of time myself at the loft, helping out with the apprentices and Mary looking after the business side of things, as well as caring for their two children, William and Margaret. He's hardly ever there and, when he is, he is either drugged or drunk. I don't know what will come of him." The old man stopped speaking, clearly upset. Isaac tried to comfort William, but it was hard to find the right words. They eventually lapsed into silence, both thinking of how things had turned out. Eventually, William broke the silence.

"Look now, lad. This is supposed to be a joyous occasion. Here's me burdening you with all my problems. Come, let us find your lovely wife and daughters and get back into the right mood again." With that, William rose from his seat, took Isaac by the arm, and led him back to the rest of the family.

*   *   *   *   *

Spring came and with it the change to the New Year. Isaac's business was doing well and he needed at times to employ additional help. He was not yet ready to pay anyone else permanently, but could offer work to journeymen sail-makers, so-called because they were paid by the day. He found that he was picking up orders that would normally have gone to Nicholas and his two former apprentices, Stephen Magnus and Mathew Fisher, were among those looking for work. Their place at the old sail loft had been taken by two new apprentices, Thomas Burch and Thomas Tilson. Burch had come to sail-making at an older age than most apprentices, as he had already served time at sea as a sailor on merchant ships.

As spring moved on to summer, Elizabeth again became pregnant and, once more, Isaac's hopes rose. His life was falling into place quite well. He had a good business, excellent contacts and a growing reputation through his position as constable for the ward, a loving wife and a growing family. He just needed the one thing to make his life complete; a son.

The months leading up to the birth in February seemed to drag by. His work and civic duties kept him busy, but he was also impatient for his new child to arrive. His two eldest daughters, Sarah and Judith, were now old enough to enjoy the annual Mart and so the family went in early February to the Tuesday Market Place to enjoy the festivities. As they wandered around the stalls and took in all the entertainment, Isaac thought back to that earlier Mart, when he had proposed marriage to Elizabeth; so much had happened to him since then. But he had little time for this reverie, as Elizabeth suddenly gave a small cry.

"What is it?" asked Isaac, anxiously.

"I'm having pains. I think it has started. Let's make our way home."

Despite the obvious disappointment of his daughters at having to leave the delights of the Mart, Isaac and his family did just that. Luckily Isaac found the midwife was at home and Elizabeth was hurried up to the bedroom, whilst Isaac looked after the rest of the family by the fireplace downstairs.

Elizabeth's labour was not as long as on previous occasions and, after only a couple of anxious hours, Isaac heard the cry of the newborn baby coming from upstairs. After another ten minutes, the midwife came to the top of the stairs and called for him to come up. Carrying Susanna, and followed by his other daughters, he quickly climbed the stairs. There he found Elizabeth lying in bed, their new child in her arms. She looked up and said with a smile, "My dear Isaac, it's a boy. We have a son." Isaac sat on the edge of the bed and took the child gently into his arms. He looked down at the small face, apparently asleep, and felt an overwhelming sense of joy and fulfilment. A tear ran down his cheek, as he pronounced the name they had decided upon.

"Welcome to the world, William."

Chapter Eleven: A Time of Death

The celebration of William's birth continued for some time. As on previous occasions, there was a family gathering at the *Eight Bells* after the christening. Once again, Nicholas was missing and Isaac sought out old William to find out more. William told him that Nicholas's illness was getting worse and he spent much of his time confined to his bed. He was even considering consulting a physician, rather than rely on the advice of an apothecary. Isaac realised that this would indeed be a serious step, as a physician would not be cheap. For someone such as Nicholas to pay for the services of a physician would be quite a drain on the finances of his sail loft. Isaac resolved to visit Nicholas soon, to see for himself how ill he had become.

In addition to the family gathering, Isaac also stood his friends drinks at the *Prince of Wales*, which was his preferred tavern. As well as Daniel Locust, Isaac had also become quite good friends with Stephen Allen junior, the son of his landlord. Stephen, at 25, was nine years younger than Isaac, but was a pleasant companion socially. He had followed his father's trade and served his apprenticeship as a wine merchant. Isaac realised that Stephen represented the future of the Allen business and was not blind to the advantages of maintaining this friendship. The Allen's had interests in several ships and this fleet could expand with their business. They would always need sails for these ships, Isaac thought.

True to his intentions, Isaac made a visit to see Nicholas. He had tried to find him at the sail loft, but he wasn't there; his father William was minding the business and watching over the two apprentices. The loft did not seem that busy and there was only one other journeyman sail-maker at work that day. After a brief conversation, Isaac left and made his way to Nicholas's house. He was greeted by a rather distraught Mary, who told Isaac how worried she was for him. As had been suggested, they had been visited a few times by a physician, who had prescribed a foul-smelling medicine, bled Nicholas, and charged ten shillings for each visit. As far as Mary could see, there had been no improvement in Nicholas's condition. She showed Isaac to the bedroom.

Nicholas lay on the bed, fully dressed, but obviously very ill. He clutched a blood-soaked handkerchief, into which he would cough every few seconds. He looked considerably thinner than the last time that Isaac had seen him and the skin that was visible was covered in sweat. Isaac realised that Nicholas was probably suffering from consumption. He also knew this to be quite serious and, not wanting to contract it himself, or carry it back to his family, he placed a chair some distance from the bed and kept his own handkerchief, in the folds of which he held an open vinaigrette containing some pungent smelling salts, close to his nose.

They talked for a while. It was a painfully slow conversation, as Nicholas had great difficulty saying more than a few words without coughing and his voice was very weak. He was a shadow of the man with whom Isaac had grown up and enjoyed so many good times together. Isaac did his best to comfort him and be cheerful, but Nicholas seemed resigned to the fact that he was unlikely to recover. His thoughts were mainly for Mary and their son, William. He asked Isaac to do what he could to see that the sail loft continued to support his family, to which Isaac readily agreed. When it came time to leave, Isaac wondered if he would see his friend again, but, in fact, he did visit Nicholas a number of times in the weeks ahead, as the illness ran its course. Nicholas clung to life into the summer, but, at the end of July, Isaac received the news of his death.

*   *   *   *   *

On the first day of August, Nicholas's family and friends assembled at the Quaker Meeting House, where a few years before Nicholas had wed Mary. As Isaac was to discover, a Quaker funeral was very much like any other Quaker service. He had agreed to act as pall-bearer for his friend and, together with William junior, Stephen Magnus, Mathew Fisher and two others, had carried the plain wooden coffin into the room and placed it on a trestle at the front of the seating. As during the wedding, much of the service was conducted in silence, with members of the congregation standing up when they felt moved, and sharing their thoughts with the rest. Many spoke of his work for the Society of Friends, as he had been an active member, not only in King's Lynn, but also throughout the county of Norfolk. He had been very involved with the acquiring of land for Quaker Burial Grounds. Eventually, his father rose to speak.

"It is always sad when a parent has to bury a son. I had expected to see Nicholas continue my business as a sail-maker, so that, when it was my time to depart this life, I could be happy that it was in safe hands. I have always been proud of my children and what they have achieved. One of the things I didn't understand with Nicholas was his becoming a Quaker. But having had many talks with him about it, as well as meeting a lot of the people here today, I am beginning to understand more. I know why it is also called the Society of Friends, because Nicholas could always rely on his friends to support him and I thank you all for that. I now want to know more, so you will be seeing much more of me at your meetings. Again, thank you."

At this point, William was clearly getting emotional and had to resume his seat. His words were followed by a long period of silence. Isaac had been taken by surprise at his closing comments, for William had always been a staunch supporter of the Established Church.

After a few more contributions, including a moving tribute from his elder brother, Isaac felt that he could not let the moment pass without sharing his own feelings. He stood up.

"I have known Nicholas since I was apprenticed to his father. He was like a brother to me, as was William, and I was always made to feel part of the family. We learned our trade together and also were great friends outside the workplace. Later, we worked alongside each other, until I set up my own loft. Although we didn't see so much of each other, I knew he would always be ready to help and support me. I would like to say to Mary, his wife, that she can now depend on my support, should she need it. His final illness came as a great shock to me, but I would like to say to you all today that I am grateful for this chance to share my feelings about Nicholas." Turning towards the coffin, Isaac finished with a simple statement of fact, "Nicholas, friend and brother, I will miss you." Isaac sat down with a heavy heart, but he also felt glad that he had had the chance to say what he had. William junior, who was sitting alongside him, reached across and gave his hand a squeeze.

As the service moved towards its conclusion, one of the overseers read a piece written by William Penn, a prominent member of the Society of Friends in the seventeenth century, and the founder of the Province of Pennsylvania.

And this is the Comfort of the Good,
That the grave cannot hold them,
And that they live as soon as they die.
For Death is no more
Than a turning of us over from time to eternity.
Death, then, being the way and condition of Life,
We cannot love to live,
If we cannot bear to die.

They that love beyond the World, cannot be separated by it.
Death cannot kill what never dies.
Nor can Spirits ever be divided
That love and live in the same Divine Principle,
The Root and Record of their Friendship.
If Absence be not death, neither is theirs.

Death is but Crossing the World, as Friends do the Seas ...

After a further period of silence, the overseers rose and shook each other's hand, signalling the end of the service. Isaac and the other pall-bearers took up the coffin and carried it outside, where a cart was waiting to take it to its final resting place. This was to be a Quaker site, known as the Old Burial Ground. Most burials at this time were carried out at the New Ground, but Nicholas's prominent position within the Society meant that he had been allocated one of the few plots remaining, near to his infant daughters, who had pre-deceased him. At the graveside, little was said as his coffin was lowered into the ground. Each of those who had followed the coffin to the grave threw a handful of earth into the grave, before leaving the final filling-in to be done by the gravediggers. As he moved away and headed back to town, Isaac reflected that Nicholas's life had not been a long one, but today's meeting had shown how much he had meant to a lot of people.

*   *   *   *   *

In the weeks that followed the funeral, Isaac had a number of meetings with Mary Elstobb and her father-in-law, to decide on the best way for the sail loft to continue. Isaac also met with the apprentices and was able to gauge their strengths and weaknesses. Between them they formulated a plan. Although Mary would continue to run the business, it was recognised that she did not have the contacts amongst the merchants and ships' masters to negotiate successfully for new work. Many of them would have found difficulty dealing with a woman in business, whilst others would take advantage of her inexperience. Isaac agreed to act as negotiator for both sail lofts and would share out the work according to the capabilities of the two establishments. He would be paid a commission on the work that he found for Mary. Mary would keep the accounts for her loft and keep the profits, from which she would help to support old William. As well as the two apprentices, who were nearing the end of their training, it was agreed that Mathew Fisher would be given permanent employment at Mary's loft, whilst Stephen Magnus would continue as a journeyman and would go to whichever loft had the most need of him at the time. All were agreed that this arrangement was beneficial to everybody.

At about the same time, Henry Crow the elder approached Isaac on behalf of another ship's master, Griffith Jenkins, who had a son coming up to fourteen in a few months. Isaac agreed to take on John Jenkins and indentures were drawn up and submitted to the council, although the new apprentice would not actually start at the loft until the following February. Henry Crow also offered to lodge the young man at his tenement, alongside his own son, so Isaac did not have to add to his crowded household. It was as well to have an extra pair of hands, for Isaac had a good reputation as a sail-maker and received a lot of work as a result. He would now have to make sure that the same quality of work came out of Mary's loft.

*   *   *   *   *

There was always an undercurrent of minor crime, usually perpetrated by those who were in poor circumstances. Usually this amounted to petty theft, especially in the market places, where those driven by circumstance would steal goods from the stalls, or pick the pockets and steal the purses of the better off. Isaac experienced this in his time as constable. More serious crimes were rarer. One reason was the harshness of the punishments meted out to those found guilty of crimes. For example, a man convicted of assault against another citizen was sentenced to a year in jail and, in addition, was publicly whipped in the Tuesday Market Place, once before the start of his sentence and then again at its conclusion.

In the October following Nicholas's death, Isaac, who was coming to the end of his term as constable, became involved in an infamous case. He was on a night patrol with a constable from the neighbouring ward, John Wardale, when they heard a commotion in one of the houses. They could hear an old man's voice crying out for help, together with the screams of a child. Then a young man, in his mid-twenties, ran out of a house, with a large blood-stained knife in his hand. Isaac recognised him at once, as he had been in trouble many times before, as Charles Holditch. He also realised that the house actually belonged to his father. Charles had been reported by his father on previous occasions for stealing goods and money from him, but had always left town before he could be arrested. Now he was back.

Surprised at being confronted in the early hours of the morning, Holditch turned to run from the two constables, but Isaac chased after him and, coming close behind him, seized hold of him, wrapping his arms around his upper body to prevent him wielding the knife. Isaac's companion then felled Holditch with a blow from his billystick and, before he could recover his senses, he was disarmed and lodged in a cell in the gaol, where he would remain until his trial.

Holditch was arraigned at the Quarter Sessions in January, before the Mayor, John Goodwyn, the Recorder, Henry Partridge, and several justices of the peace. Isaac and his companion gave their evidence of the arrest, whilst the father described the events of the night. Charles Holditch had entered the house shortly after one in the morning, intent on robbing the old man. His father had woken up and disturbed him, at which point the young man attacked him with the knife he was carrying. Although he had wounded his father, with a cut to the right forearm, he was further disturbed by the screams of a small boy, who was sleeping in the same room and who had woken at the commotion. At this point, Holditch decided to flee, but his escape was foiled by the two constables.

Faced with such overwhelming evidence, Holditch broke down and admitted his crimes. There could be only one sentence. He was returned to the gaol, whilst a gallows was prepared on the common in South Lynn, near the South Gate. His execution was set for the 14th of February, towards the end of the annual Mart, so, with so many people enjoying a break from work, a large crowd would be there to witness the execution. As someone who had had a hand in the arrest of the doomed man, Isaac was commanded by the court to attend the execution. He also decided to close the loft for the day, so that his workers could witness a salutary lesson in the consequences of crime.

Isaac, Daniel and the two apprentices, made their way to South Lynn. When they arrived, there was already a large crowd gathered in anticipation of what was, to many of them, expected to be an entertaining spectacle. Isaac and the others made their way towards the site of the gallows. Isaac knew that the court officials would all be there to witness the sentence being carried out and, as one of the town's constables and a constable and witness in the case, he could take his place with them, together with his companions.

At the appointed time, Holditch was brought from the gaol in a cart, along with a coffin. It was later reported that he had appeared to fall into some kind of seizure or fit no less than six times in his journey to the common, but seemed to have recovered his composure by the time he reached the site of the gallows. He received a mixed reception from the crowd. Most disapproved of his crime against his own father and there was a chorus of boos and catcalls, together with a few missiles being thrown. These were mostly rotten vegetables, or handfuls of horse manure, but were generally ineffective, as the main part of the crowd was kept back some distance from the gallows by the town's Redcoats. There were others in the crowd who were more sympathetic, being moved by the sight of such a young man being sent to his death, and these called out words of encouragement to face his end bravely, together with suitable Biblical quotations.

A minister said prayers and the choir from All Saints Church sang the Lamentation for Sinners. Then the minister asked Holditch if he wished to say anything, before being executed. From a sitting position in the cart, he gave a heartfelt plea to all young men present to learn from his example and not to follow a life of crime, which was greeted with sympathetic applause from sections of the crowd. Then he removed his jacket and was helped to stand on the coffin, while the rope was put around his neck. In his left hand he held a large handkerchief. Once more he turned to the crowd and repeated his fervent warnings not to follow his way of life, but to pay heed to the advice given by the Reverend Thomas Pyle in his many "fire and brimstone" sermons in St Margaret's Church. Then he commenced to pray loudly, calling for forgiveness and the salvation of his miserable soul. The crowd fell silent at this, as he now seemed reconciled to his impending death. At length, he stopped, dropped the handkerchief and jumped off the coffin towards the back of the cart, which was greeted by a loud shout from the crowd. The driver of the cart, seeing the signal from the handkerchief, whipped the horses into life and drove away, leaving the poor unfortunate man suspended at the end of the rope, twisting and kicking, as the breath was squeezed out of him. .

Although the man's struggles at the end of the rope lasted only a few minutes, before it was obvious to all that he was dead, his body was left hanging for about half an hour, before being lowered, checked by a physician, and placed in the coffin. It was then taken to St Margaret's

Church, where it was buried in an unmarked grave. No record was made in the parish register.

Many of the crowd would now return to the pleasures of the Mart, or gather in the taverns to discuss what they had seen, but Isaac, Daniel Locust and the two apprentices walked back to the loft. They scarcely spoke on the way there and the mood was quite solemn. Whilst Daniel was familiar with death in many forms from his time at sea, the two boys were not, and Isaac hoped that what they had witnessed would help keep them honest in the future.

*   *   *   *   *

Isaac's reputation as a skilled craftsman and a good master continued to attract those wishing to learn the trade. In late March, just after Lady's Day and the change of the year to 1751, he was approached on behalf of Sir William Browne M.D., to take on the son, Samuel Browne, of a recently deceased relative, Richard Browne. Sir William was a prominent physician and member of the College of Physicians. He had come to Lynn some thirty years earlier, under the patronage of the Turner family, and had made quite a fortune practising as a physician in the town. He had left Lynn about two years ago to move to London, in order to gain his due place in his profession. During his time in Lynn, he had had a reputation as a ladies' man, as was shown by the following verse, originally written in Latin (some say by Sir William himself):

> *Be thou, O knight, the giant's scourge and dread,*
> *Who night and day preys on the victim maid.*
> *Herculean labour Lerna's monsters slew,*
> *Oh! may thy labours those of Lynn subdue.*

Sir William was offering to pay the customary ten guineas towards the boy's apprenticeship himself and Isaac, sensing that helping such a prominent man would not do him any harm, agreed to take on the boy. One of the downstairs rooms at his tenement was equipped with a bed and Samuel moved in with the Forster family.

*　　*　　*　　*　　*

Whilst Isaac continued to build his business and assist with his old loft, events were happening, both in King's Lynn itself and nationally, that would have an influence on himself and his family. In late March of 1751, the news came from London that Frederick, the Prince of Wales, whose wedding the town had so joyously celebrated in 1736, had died. The cause of death was a burst abscess on his lung. It was commonly reported that the abscess had been caused by him being struck in the chest by a cricket ball, cricket being a game for which he had great enthusiasm. He had also taken a great interest in politics and it was his support for the Tory opposition that had led his father, who was widely known not to like his son, to call the snap election in 1747. The opposition had lost that election to the Whigs and Frederick's influence had waned. It was perhaps because of this that the greatest sense of loss amongst the citizens of King's Lynn was felt by the supporters of William Folkes, of whom Isaac had been one.

Rents were traditionally paid on the Quarter Days during the year and, on Midsummer's Day, the 24th June, Isaac duly went to Stephen Allen's offices, in the south wing of Hampton Court, to pay his dues. On arrival, he was a little surprised to find Stephen junior making the collections. Naturally, he asked after the father's well-being. Young Stephen was not his usual cheerful self and looked concerned as he replied.

"I'm afraid he's not well. He has been struck down with a fever, which shows no sign of abating."

"Is he receiving good care?" asked Isaac.

"Oh, yes. His friend and fellow councillor, Doctor Joseph Taylor, is visiting him often, but whatever he tries seems to have little effect."

"Please wish him well from me. He has been a good friend to me and my family. I hope we will see him again soon."

Alas, Isaac's wishes were not fulfilled. The wine merchant died at the end of August and Isaac was amongst those attending his funeral at St

Margaret's on the 4th of September. After that, his friend, young Stephen, would be his new landlord.

*   *   *   *   *

The year 1751 had begun on March 26th, following Lady's Day on the 25th, but this would be the last time that the New Year would be officially celebrated at this time of the year. The Calendar Act of 1750, which had been steered through Parliament principally by Philip Stanhope, the fourth Earl of Chesterfield (and was consequently often referred to as the Chesterfield Act), paved the way for the adoption in Britain and its colonies of the Gregorian Calendar. Up until this point, the Julian Calendar had been used in this country. As long ago as 1582, Pope Gregory XIII had ordered that the calendar be changed in order to return the celebration of Easter to the time of the year agreed upon at the First Council of Nicaea in 325. This had required a change in the calendar of ten days, so that the spring equinox again fell on March 21st, and, in order to maintain this more accurately and prevent another gradual drift away from the correct relationship, a change in the system of extra days in leap years was needed. In the Gregorian calendar, leap years were not to be used in centennial years that were not divisible by four hundred. Thus, while 1600 had been a leap year, 1700 had not.

Initially, the calendar was only adopted by Catholic countries, who naturally obeyed the Papal Bull, with Protestant and Orthodox countries retaining the old calendar. Eventually, most countries did make the switch and Britain was amongst the last of the European countries to do so.

As a result of these changes, 1751 would be a very short year, ending on the 31st December, whilst New Year's Day for 1752 would now be on January 1st. Although Scotland was also using the Julian Calendar up until this time, it had actually changed to using January 1st as the start of the year in 1600. This often led to confusion when official deeds and contracts were drawn up between traders from England and Scotland. The other part of the change made necessary by the new calendar was to adjust the date to accommodate what had now become an eleven day discrepancy between the two systems. As a result, people in Britain and its colonies went to sleep on the 2nd September 1752 and woke up, the very next day, on the 14th September. The intervening eleven days had been omitted.

Many people were confused about this loss of eleven days. Some thought that they had actually lost eleven days of their life, whilst others, whose birthdays fell between these dates, felt aggrieved at that. Some saw it as a political move and, at a later election in Oxford, this was seized upon by the Tory opposition as an issue with which to berate the Whig candidate. Much more relevant to those who paid rent and taxes was the fact that the next Quarter Day was now due eleven days earlier than expected. However, the Act had foreseen this and due adjustments were made by all but the most unscrupulous of landlords. Nationally, the end of the tax year was put back from Lady's Day on the 25th March to the 5th April.

Meanwhile, Isaac continued with his sail-making, training his apprentices, and looking after his family. In 1752, his eldest daughter, Sarah, was nine years old, Judith was eight, Susanna three, and his son, William, was two. Isaac, in spite of all that happened to others in recent years, had every reason to feel content with his lot.

Chapter Twelve: Education and Service

On the 10th July 1754, Isaac had the pleasure of accompanying the first of his apprentices, Henry Crow, to the Guildhall, to see him sworn in as a freeman of the town on the completion of his apprenticeship. However, Henry did not continue in Isaac's employ for long. As had long been expected, he decided to join his father on his ship. It was barely a month later that the elder Henry's ship returned to port and young Henry took his leave of the sail loft. The father was proud that his son had finished his apprenticeship and acquired skills that would be useful on board ship and invited Isaac and the others in the sail loft to join him for a few drinks, before he set off, now with his son at his side, on his next voyage.

This journey to the Guildhall brought back memories of when he had gone there with his master to take the oath of a freeman of the town. Isaac had always kept in touch with William Elstobb, now in his eighties. Since the death of Nicholas, things had changed for William. Although he still received a small income from the sail-making business, he had lost money when he acted as a guarantor for a loan. He decided that, with just himself and Margaret left together, they would move to a smaller house and now rented a single floor in a house on London Road, which was owned by the Quakers, having been left in trust to them by Thomas Buckingham. Buckingham had been a wealthy merchant and philanthropist, who had died early in the century. Although a staunch member of the Society of Friends, he nevertheless took a full part in local affairs, taking on the duties of overseer of the poor, distributing parish relief to the needy, on several occasions.

Isaac often visited William there, when he and Elizabeth came to visit her family at the *Eight Bells*. Then, in October 1755, came the sad news that Margaret had died. True to his word at Nicholas' funeral, William had continued with the Quakers and Isaac found himself once more attending a Quaker funeral on the 6th October. During the time that Isaac had been with the Elstobbs, Margaret had been like a mother to him, so he felt her passing as much as if she had been his real mother.

*　　*　　*　　*　　*

Earlier that year, Isaac had received a visit at the loft from Stephen Allen. His friend had been invited by the Aldermen to take his late father's place as a Common Councillor and it was in this capacity that he now wanted to speak to Isaac. Like the older Stephen Allen before him, he had come to recruit Isaac to civic duty. This time he wanted Isaac to be one of the headboroughs for the ward. At first Isaac was not too keen. He remembered the year he had spent as constable and how it had eaten into his time. But Stephen was quite persuasive.

"Come now, Isaac," he began, "seven years ago your business was just still in its early life and your apprentice had only just started. Now he is fully qualified and you have your other sail-maker, Daniel, whilst John Jenkins has only a short time to go before he finishes his apprenticeship as well. Between them and young Samuel Browne, you know you can trust them to keep the loft going without you being there all the time."

Isaac had to admit that this was all true; he already spent quite a while going round drumming up business for both himself and Mary Elstobb, as well as arranging delivery of the raw materials of their trade. He had left Daniel in charge in the loft and the former mariner, with the sense of discipline instilled in him by the Royal Navy, had never let him down.

Stephen continued, "Look, I have been headborough myself for the past year. I need to take a break at the moment, as I'm forming a business partnership with George Hogge and this is taking a lot of my time. However, I promise that I will offer myself as one of the headboroughs next year. Perhaps we'll both be there – what a team we'd make."

Isaac capitulated. "How can I refuse you, when you put it like that. You can submit my name to the Leet Court."

Since it was almost the end of the working day, Isaac dismissed the remainder of those working in the loft. Then he and Stephen went to the *Prince of Wales* to toast this new duty in a few tankards of ale.

Isaac's previous experience as a constable for the Stonegate ward had given him some insight into the work of the headboroughs, but he now found out more concerning their duties. Originally, in mediaeval times, a headborough had been a person responsible for the behaviour of a group of ten households; he acted as their head man and representative within the community. King's Lynn had retained the ancient name, but, with a greatly increased population, each of the ten wards of the town had two headboroughs and a constable. Many minor infractions in the town were originally dealt with by the Leet Court, but, whilst the Leet Court remained as the body that administered the constables, headboroughs and other minor officials, the judicial side had become merged with the Guildhall Court, under the jurisdiction of the Mayor and other Aldermen. This court dealt with all manner of relatively minor matters, such as the settling of disputes, or the maintenance of the standard of goods sold in shops, markets and taverns. Anyone found to be supplying inferior quality of produce, or selling short measure, could be summoned before the court and fined. The Leet Court itself still met every October to elect and swear in the constables and headboroughs for each ward.

Thus it was that Isaac found himself, on the 28th October, standing with all the others about to take office before the Steward, Robert Underwood, and the Mayor, William Langley, and hearing the Steward intone the ancient oath of a headborough.

"Sirs, you shall truly enquire and due presentment make of all such matters, articles and things that are inquirable in the Leet. The King's counsel, your fellows' and your own you shall truly keep. You shall present nothing for malice or evil, nor conceal anything for mood, dread, favour, affection, or corruption, but present the truth in all things, as near as God will give you grace. "

All the headboroughs replied in unison, "So God me help."

The constables and other officials were similarly sworn in.

At the conclusion of the ceremony, the Mayor and the Steward, accompanied by the town's four Sergeants-at-Mace and the Bailiff, left the assembly room of the Guildhall, followed by the Aldermen and Councillors, who had been there as witnesses. Then the various constables and headboroughs also left, usually, like Isaac, to enjoy a chat over a tankard at a local tavern.

The constable for the Stonegate ward was one Robert Massam, a cooper, whilst the other headborough was Daniel Sergeant, a blacksmith. Isaac knew both of them as neighbours, but had little to do with them through business. Now, over a tankard of beer in the *Prince of Wales*, he started to find out more about them. After some persuasion by Stephen Allen, Isaac was now a headborough. Little did he realise it at the time, but he would serve in this position for the next nine years.

*   *   *   *   *

Isaac was always keen to provide the best for his family. With the business doing well and the household finances on a firm footing, he determined that all his children would have a good education. It was often the case that the daughters in a family would not receive much in the way of formal education. It was considered sufficient to train them in the skills of running a home and only a third of women at the time could even sign their name. However, Isaac was not of this mind; he wished his daughters to get a good start in life that would equip them to raise their station as they grew older. Consequently, he sent them all in their turn to the town's English School, where they could learn to read and write correctly. In addition, Elizabeth would teach them many skills about the house, whilst they also had tutoring in skills such as sewing, embroidery and knitting.

Young William's education was to be much broader and directed to being in business one day. He would not only be taught to read and write, but would also have lessons in mathematics, geography, accounting, law, business correspondence and many other topics. In addition, he had some tutoring in Latin, given by one of the local priests. This was to qualify him to take a place at the Free, or grammar, School, since Isaac, being a freeman of the town, was entitled to have his son educated gratis at this school. Isaac wished William to be well educated by the time he reached an age when he could begin his apprenticeship.

In 1756 a series of events were to take place that would have an influence on the Forster family. The first of these centred round William Elstobb the Younger. Since the election of 1747, where he had been a strong supporter of Sir John Turner, William's fortunes, unlike those of his father, had taken a turn for the better, thanks to the patronage he now enjoyed from Sir John and other Aldermen. He had spent some time as Chamberlain to the Town Council, looking after the town's accounts and also acting as the town's Surveyor of the Waterways, which naturally paid a good stipend and offered opportunities to further his business contacts. Then, in February 1756, he was made Master of the English School, following the death of the precious incumbent, Thomas Robotom. In return for educating three poor children, nominated by the Mayor, he had the use of the school premises rent free. All other pupils that were sent to the school were paid for by their parents and this provided William with a useful income, even after employing an additional teacher to assist him. By this time, Sarah and Judith were approaching the end of their schooling and would normally have been expected to leave and find employment, but the new Master of the school offered them both positions as assistants, helping to teach the younger children to read and write. It was quite common at the time for the older children to help with the schooling in this way, but it was also excellent preparation for them to become full-time teachers, or even governesses in a private family, at a later date.

Later in the year, towards the end of April, William was also commissioned by the Mayor, William Langley, and Corporation to carry out a survey of Snettisham Farm, which was a large property of over three hundred acres, owned by the town and situated some ten or eleven miles north east of King's Lynn. This often kept him out of the school for many hours and, under the overall control of the deputy teacher, Sarah and Judith found themselves kept busy with the younger children.

Whilst it was not always easy, it was something that they both enjoyed and for which they showed an aptitude.

*   *   *   *   *

Isaac found the duties of headborough to be quite interesting. As well as his duties in checking the quality of goods on offer at the markets, testing weights and measures, and assisting the constable to keep order around the ward, particularly at the Saturday Market Place, he was also required to attend the Guildhall Court every other Wednesday, where a variety of minor matters were dealt with. The jury that would hear these cases, and decide on their outcome, would be drawn from the headboroughs. With ten wards and, therefore, twenty headboroughs to choose from, Isaac would not be needed every time, but was still expected to be at the Guildhall for the start of the day. Indeed, the court would levy fines on any of them that did not arrive on time, ranging from two-pence if they were not present at the last stroke of the clock, up to five shillings, if a whole session was missed. Isaac was always careful with his money and made a point of always being at the Guildhall early.

Most of the cases that came before the Guildhall Court were relatively minor, as the more serious cases would be dealt with at the Quarter Sessions. Many were minor disputes between neighbours, particularly where a debt was involved. The plaintiff in the case would normally be represented by a lawyer, usually one of Mr Debenham, Mr Bland, or Mr Case, whilst the defendants would use the services of Mr Rollett, Mr Lyther, or Mr Stream. Isaac noticed that most of the town's Sergeants at Mace were drawn from the ranks of these advocates. Each side would present their arguments, any witnesses would be heard, then the jury would deliver a verdict. Additional Leet Court officials, known as affeerors, would have assessed the level of any fines or damages to be imposed on the loser in the case.

The whole process was conducted at a brisk pace, and a dozen or more cases would be dealt with in a single session. Jury deliberations were generally made without leaving the court, being simply a quick consultation. Whilst most of the cases were of a fairly mundane nature,

Isaac was told by another headborough, who had served the previous year, of the case of Hannah Clark. She had been found guilty of being a common scold and sentenced to be ducked. The town's ducking stool was to be found by the Purfleet and the unfortunate woman was immersed in the filthy waters of this outlet into the river several times, much to the entertainment and amusement of a large crowd that had gathered to watch. Most expected that her husband would have a more peaceful time after that.

True to his word, Stephen Allen became headborough the following year. Isaac decided to continue with him, whilst the constable for the ward was now John Blade. John had a shop on the north-west corner of Priory Lane, where he was a block-maker. He fashioned individual blocks modelled on the heads of his customers, so that they could get their wigs and hats made to exactly the right size. Both Stephen and Allen were among his customers.

The ensuing months would prove to be difficult for the town in general and, in particular, also for those, like Isaac, Stephen and John, who helped to keep order in the town. The winter at the start of 1757 was abnormally cold, to the extent that the river was frozen and the port was closed. This led to severe shortages of food, especially bread, and widespread unemployment. Isaac's own business was quiet, with virtually no money coming in. However, this was not unexpected at this time of year, as the peak demand for new sails would be in the spring and summer, when new ships would be commissioned from the shipyards. Like a squirrel storing nuts for winter, Isaac had kept back a large proportion of his income from the previous year, so he was able to keep all his sail-makers and apprentices on during these times, building up a stock of finished sails for when business picked up. He was fortunate that the local shipbuilders built their ships to common patterns, so Isaac did not have to guess at the dimensions of the sails that would be needed.

Matters were not so fortunate in the town, however, with groups of idle men wandering the streets, fomenting trouble. Petty crime increased and Isaac spent more time away from the loft in order to try to prevent this. Naturally enough, the mayor and corporation were very concerned about this. They distributed coal free of charge to the population of the town. All the leading merchants in the town, recognising the benefits to their businesses of a contented population, were supporters of local charities and the money from these was used to provide for the poor during these hard times. One factor in the shortage of bread was the fact that a lot of the available wheat and barley was used for distilling spirits, so the corporation decided to petition Parliament for an Act to stop this. Two years later such an Act was indeed passed.

The shortages of wheat for flour continued throughout the year, driving prices ever upwards. One of the leading merchants, George Hogge, offered to lend the town a £1000 to help relieve the situation. With this money, the corporation commissioned Stephen Allen, now Hogge's partner in business, and another merchant, named Alderson, to send ships along the coast to Hull, in order to get more stocks of wheat. Some of this was sold to the town bakers at a reasonable price, whilst other money was raised from the richer inhabitants to allow flour to be sold to the poor at half the current price. Such acts of charity were welcomed by those needing them most and probably prevented serious rioting from breaking out, as had been seen in other parts of the country.

*　　*　　*　　*　　*

Isaac quite enjoyed the responsibility of being headborough. He felt that he was contributing something to the community and, in return, was gaining the respect of his fellow citizens, as well as the beneficial side-effects of contacts with the more influential merchants in the town. John Blade and Stephen Allen had proved to be good friends and companions, so Isaac was quite pleased when they all agreed to continue together for another year.

In the May of 1758, John Jenkins completed his apprenticeship and, like Henry Crow before him, decided that a life at sea, sailing under his father, was where his future lay. At first this left Isaac short-handed at the loft, but this problem was solved when Mary Elstobb decided to sell the old Elstobb business. She did offer it to Isaac, but he felt that running his own loft would be more than enough for him. At this point, Daniel

Locust admitted to having a sizeable amount of money left from the prize money he had gained during the latter days of his naval service. He took over the business, keeping on Thomas Burch to assist him, whilst Isaac employed Thomas Tilson in his loft. The two old seafarers were likely to make a good pairing, keeping each other amused, as they tried to out-do each other with wild tales of their days at sea. Isaac had had a chance, during the time that he was bringing in work for both lofts, to see the standard of Thomas Tilson's work and was sure that he would make a good addition to his own loft. Samuel Browne was also nearing the end of his term and Isaac decided that he would also employ him. He had already taken on another apprentice, Edward Barrett, in February. He calculated that this would fill the gap nicely, before his son William would be ready to start his training. By keeping a couple of apprentices in the loft, who could do many of the menial tasks, Isaac could keep down his costs and also keep the more experienced sail-makers more gainfully employed.

Once again in October the constables and headboroughs were elected and sworn in at the Leet Court. Isaac agreed to continue, but Stephen's health was giving him problems and he was finding it hard even to maintain attendance at council meetings, so he decided to step aside. His place was taken by a local carpenter, William Tyson. John Blade continued as constable for a third year, although this was to be his last year in the post.

*   *   *   *   *

In the third week of May of 1759, the traditional Perambulation of the parish boundaries took place. Each year, parishioners would spend a day, which would be one of the Rogation Days just before Ascension Day, walking round the boundaries of their parish. Whilst not everyone would take part in this walk, it was expected that boys of around the age of ten would be there, to learn the extent of the parish in which they lived. Because of this, William was "invited" to join the Perambulation; it was not so much an invitation that he could refuse, as a duty that was placed on him, as a rite of passage. If William had heard what awaited him that day, he did not say, whilst Isaac, remembering his own initial

Perambulation in South Lynn, many years previously, also kept his own counsel.

Wednesday, the 23rd May, had been the date chosen for the walk and proved to be a good choice, as the weather was fine and the sun was shining. Early in the morning, William was taken by Isaac to the door of the church, where he joined a group of about a dozen boys of similar age. Because of the warm weather, he was dressed simply in his shirt and a pair of old breeches, as well as some sturdy shoes. Isaac had advised him to go without stockings and he saw that the other boys were dressed similarly. Isaac would not be joining him on the walk, as he was busy with the loft and his other duties as headborough, so he left him there, under the supervision of the Reverend Charles Bagge, the current vicar of St Margaret's.

The previous vicar of both St Margaret's and All Saints had been Thomas Pyle, but he had retired, due to ill health, in 1755 and had died at the end of the following year. He had been buried at All Saints. Whilst Thomas Pyle had been vicar at St Margaret's, All Saints and St Nicholas' Chapel, the duties had been split between two new incumbents, Charles Bagge at St Margaret's and St Nicholas', whilst All Saints was now the responsibility of Charles Phelpes.

The day started with a short service, at which the Reverend Bagge used a short extract from his sermon of the previous Sunday, which he had taken from the second *Book of Homilies*, sermons dating back to Tudor times, but which vicars still found useful at this time for particular occasions.

"We have occasion given us in our walks to-day, to consider the old ancient bounds and limits belonging to our township and to other our neighbours bordering about us, to the intent that we should be content with our own and not contentiously strive for others, to the breach of charity, by any encroaching one upon another or claiming one of another further than in ancient right and custom our forefathers have peacefully laid out unto us for our commodity and comfort."

At the conclusion of the service, all were led outside by the vicar. Many of the parishioners were not actually taking part in the Perambulation, especially the older ones and the women, but soon the procession set off. At its head was the vicar, followed by the group of young boys, now carrying willow branches, with which they would be encouraged to "beat the bounds" as they went. Together with them were a group of sturdy young men, in their late teens or twenties, who carried young sapling branches, with the leaves and bark stripped away. A further crowd of parishioners followed, anxious for a day out in the sun and hoping for some merriment along the way. At the tail end came a horse and cart, in the charge of the churchwardens and laden with food and drink, supplied by the parish and the town.

Their walk first took them to the riverbank, where they continued in a northerly direction along the quay-sides. Whilst the locals, who worked at loading and unloading the ships at anchor, were mostly respectful, understanding the meaning of this journey, the sailors on board many of the vessels were less so, shouting out a number of, to themselves at least, humorous comments, quite a few of which were, perhaps, a bit too ribald for the ears of churchmen and young boys. The boys pretended not to notice and contented themselves with beating everything they could with their willow sticks.

They followed the river past the Purfleet and the Custom House and then on further, until they had passed to the north of St Nicholas' Chapel. Then they followed the coast round to where an inlet, being part of the River Gaywood, separated the limits of the parish from Fort Ann. The vicar called on the party to pause awhile and pointed out a low post, called a dewel, or duel, which marked the limits of the parish. He turned to the group of boys, which included William, and told them to mark it well and remember it.

Then the boys were lined up in turn by the dewel and the young men each gave them a stroke with saplings across the seat of their breeches. Some cried out with the pain of this initiation, but William was determined to bear it with fortitude, rather than lose face with his peers.

All the boys would have a good reason to remember exactly where this particular dewel was to be found.

The Perambulation continued in like manner along the edge of the river. This part of the walk was mainly along the edge of open fields and there were many ditches, used to irrigate the fields. This would cause the Reverend Bagge, the churchwardens, with their valuable load of victuals, and the more prudent of the walkers to divert to where small bridges offered a crossing point. But the young men could jump most of these with ease and would encourage the boys to do the same. Of course, some of the ditches were too wide for such young legs and William soon realised his father's wisdom in getting him to wear his oldest breeches and leaving his stockings at home, as he emerged drenched in muddy water from ditch after ditch. The young men were in a merry mood, helped by occasional raids on the cart for a drink of beer, and enjoyed playing tricks on others in the company, apart from the easy targets that were the boys. At one point, for example, one of the churchwardens, who had but recently been appointed to the post, found himself deposited in a bed of nettles. Indeed, with the obvious exception of the vicar, nearly all in the group found themselves the butt of some joke or another.

William had rarely been into the countryside, as his life revolved around the centre of King's Lynn; Hampton Court, school, church, and the markets. In spite of some obvious discomfort, he was enjoying the day. He looked across the fields of ripening corn and was particularly struck by the song of a skylark, which hovered over the fields. The air was fresh, with none of the pungent smells that were to be encountered in the streets of the town. The warmth of the sun felt good and he wished that he could spend much more time here. But the procession moved relentlessly on, as they had still a way to go.

Eventually they reached a point on the river, some two hundred paces north of the East Gate, by a kettle mill and water engine, which they were told supplied water to the town from the River Gaywood. Also at the point, causing trepidation among the boys, was another dewel. After the usual exhortation from the vicar to mark it well and remember it, the boys were again subjected to a beating from their elders, made all the more effective by their wet breeches.

After this, the company settled down to consume the contents of the cart. There were plentiful amounts of meat and bread, together with beer and wine to wash it down. The boys were allowed small beer, being a very weak brew. There were quite a few invitations from the company to the boys to "sit down and enjoy your meal", but, unsurprisingly, they preferred to remain standing.

After this, the walk continued along the path of the town walls, moving south until they passed Lady's Mount and encountered the small river that led to Ball Fleet. Then they walked back towards the river, before concluding their walk along Boal Lane and then back inland to St Margaret's Church. Unfortunately for William and his fellow initiates, they encountered another four dewels along the way, each of which left a lasting impression on their young minds, as well as elsewhere. Their only compensation would be the gift of one penny each, for their pains, when they arrived back at the church.

Isaac had known what lay in store for William, when he had left him at the church that morning. He well remembered a similar ordeal in South Lynn, when he was a similar age. When William returned home, he had every sympathy for him, although William himself was unwilling to talk much about his day, or complain at his treatment, except to comment on how he had enjoyed the time spent by the fields, the fresh air and the joy he had felt on hearing the skylark's song. He knew that all boys in the parish were expected to go through this instruction in the limits of the place to which they owed allegiance. When Isaac learnt later of his stoicism, he helped to ease his discomfort by adding another penny to that from the parish.

*   *   *   *   *

1759 proved to be a more difficult year in which to find suitable volunteers for the civic posts. Eventually Daniel Burrell, a barber and periwig maker, was persuaded to take on the post of constable and Isaac continued as headborough. As the date for the Leet Court approached, the second headborough had still to be found. Then, at Stephen Allen's suggestion, Isaac was persuaded to ask Samuel Browne to take the post. Although he was barely out of his apprenticeship and not particularly well known in the community, Samuel was, nevertheless, a well-built young man and had an imposing physical presence, that would serve him well in case of any confrontations.

Isaac had his doubts as to the suitability of the young man for such responsibilities, but let his name go forward. Whilst his nomination was reluctantly accepted by the Corporation at their Congregation on the fifth of October, by the time the Leet Court was convened on the following Monday, the ninth, Isaac had talked to someone with whom he had done a lot of business, John Hart

John Hart was a rope-maker and was a regular supplier to Isaac. They often had enjoyed a drink in each other's company and it was during a drink together on the Friday, that Isaac had suggested to John that he would make a good headborough. Remembering all the tricks of persuasion that Stephen Allen had used with him, he eventually persuaded John to agree. Actually, it wasn't that difficult. John had ambitions to exchange his life as a tradesman for that of a merchant. He knew that he would have to make the right contacts and these were mainly to be found amongst the Aldermen and Councillors. When he mentioned this to Isaac, his drinking companion agreed that such contacts had proved useful for him and would undoubtedly do so for John. Isaac later passed on this information to Stephen Allen, who agreed to contact the Mayor, Charles Turner, with the change of nominee.

The Mayor and Corporation found John Hart more to their liking than a young man, only recently time-served, and were happy to accept John Hart for the post. In fact, John was to serve a total of five years alongside Isaac. .

*   *   *   *   *

In early November 1760, news reached the town of the death of the king, George II. He had reigned since 1727, but he had not been universally popular with the people of King's Lynn. He had often been at loggerheads with their own favourite, Sir Robert Walpole, and the Walpoles, notably Sir Robert's son Horace, had spread the word that George was a buffoon and warmonger. Whilst the Corporation did their duty by attending suitable church services on the day of the late king's funeral, much of the town went about their business without showing any great feeling for the departed monarch. The bells in the churches did, however, dutifully toll for several hours.

Rumours of the manner of his death soon became the subject of tavern talk and caused a lot of ribald laughter and scatological comment. According to these stories, George had suffered a great deal from constipation. On the morning of his death, the 25th October, he had retired to his close stool, an enclosed commode, in an attempt to relieve himself. Unfortunately, the strain of his efforts proved too much for the 77 year-old's heart and he collapsed on the floor. His valet heard the crash and came to his aid, but he had died soon afterwards. The imagined scene of the king dying with his breeches around his ankles led to much amusement.

George II was succeeded by his grandson, the son of the late Prince of Wales, who ascended the throne as George III. Unlike his Hanoverian ancestors, the new king was born in England and spoke English as his first language. Even in religious matters, his education had been in the Anglican tradition. It was said that he had taken part, at the age of ten, in a family production of Joseph Addison's play Cato and had uttered the lines *"What, tho' a boy! It may with truth be said, A boy in England born, in England bred"*. This quotation became associated with him and created a favorable impression in the minds of the general population, which was enhanced in 1761, when there were not one, but two, holidays around the time of his coronation. First, on the 8th September 1761, the country celebrated his marriage to Princess Charlotte of Mecklenburg-Strelitz, to be followed a fortnight later in further celebrations of the coronation itself. All of the town was on the streets to enjoy the celebrations, which went on late into the night. The bells of St Margaret's seemed to ring almost continuously. Later in the evening, Isaac and the family went to the Tuesday Market Place to enjoy a spectacular firework display.

Isaac had partaken of his share of tavern talk about the change of monarchs and was with the majority who thought that the country had done well to swap a half-blind, nearly deaf, septuagenarian, who had spent long periods of his reign in Hanover, for a young man in his early twenties. Whilst the country was still embroiled in a war with France and Spain, later to become known as the Seven Years War, there was a new sense of hope for the country.

Chapter Thirteen: A Move to Pastures New

If 1760 marked a fresh start for the country, it was also to be a turning point for the Forster family, in particular the two eldest daughters. Sarah was now seventeen and Judith sixteen. They had been of help to Elizabeth about the house, looking after the needs of Isaac, William and the apprentices. Sarah had also spent some time in the evenings, serving at the *Prince of Wales*, but Elizabeth was only too aware of the problems of being an attractive young lady in a tavern and did not wish her daughter to continue there in the long term. Both girls had continued to help out at the school and both Isaac and Elizabeth felt that this was where their future lay. To this end, Isaac had arranged extra instruction in various subjects, to better fit them for employment in a post as a teacher or governess.

Back in 1747, Isaac had been involved with the election campaign of William Folkes and had made the acquaintance of a number of merchants in the town. It was one of these, John Fysh, who offered Isaac some help in finding a post for one of the girls. Fysh was the owner of several ships, including whalers, and had business contacts in London. He had kept in touch with William Folkes and, through him, had learnt of a good family, the Wilmots, living just south of the capital, who were in need of a governess. Isaac had fitted a number of his ships over the years and the two were well acquainted. Fysh knew of Isaac's ambitions for his daughters and suggested to him that this might be a suitable opening for one of the girls.

Isaac felt this was indeed a good opportunity and it shouldn't be missed. Persuading Elizabeth was another matter. She did not like the idea of one of her daughters moving so far away from home. It was a big step.

Isaac spent a long time with Elizabeth and the girls discussing the virtues of accepting this opportunity. He could see the drawbacks of sending one of them into a strange place, working among strangers, but he also knew that such an opportunity would be very unlikely to arise in King's

Lynn itself. Eventually, his arguments prevailed and it was decided that Sarah would be the one to be put forward for the post.

Isaac confirmed this to James Fysh, who agreed to give Sarah a character reference and to pass on his recommendation when he next visited London, which would be the following week. Within a month, Fysh had returned to King's Lynn and told Isaac that all had been agreed. The Wilmot family had agreed that Sarah would be the governess to their two young children and would expect her as soon as was convenient.

A few weeks later, the Forster family walked together on a bright summer's day to the Tuesday Market Place, where the London stage would leave from outside the *Duke's Head*. Sarah was dressed in smart new clothes, as would befit her new status, and was leading the way with Elizabeth. The rest of her belongings were packed into a large trunk, which Isaac wheeled along on a handcart. Judith, Susannah and William walked alongside the cart, glad to be away from their usual routine for a short time. James Fysh had made all the arrangements with the Wilmot family and they had agreed to meet the stage the next morning, on its arrival in London, and take Sarah on to their country house.

When they arrived at the Tuesday Market, the stage was already there and loading had commenced. It had been Isaac's intention to leave things as late as possible, as he did not wish Elizabeth and Sarah to suffer the strain of a long drawn out parting. He had secured a seat inside the stage for Sarah, and her trunk was soon hauled up onto the roof. The family had spent some time the evening previously to say all the things that they wished to say and both Isaac and Elizabeth had passed on what advice they could. It was left now for each to say their goodbyes, before Sarah climbed aboard the coach. The last words before the coach set off were from young William.

"Write soon, Sarah, and tell us all about everything." Sarah smiled and promised that she would. The coachman blew on the posthorn and the horses moved forward. The last sight of Sarah was her hand waving from the window, as the coach headed southwards along Briggate.

The family followed the same route, as they returned to Hampton Court. Elizabeth was very quiet and dabbed at her eyes with a handkerchief. Isaac left the children to pull the empty cart, as he walked alongside his wife, with a comforting arm around her shoulder. He knew that this was a wrench for Elizabeth, but he also knew that Sarah now had the promise of a fulfilling life and career, and who knew what else.

*   *   *   *   *

Nearly three weeks after Sarah had left for London, a messenger from the *Duke's Head* arrived at the sail loft. A letter had been delivered by the London stage and Isaac immediately recognised Sarah's handwriting on the letter. It was quite bulky for a letter and Isaac needed to pay two shillings and tuppence before it was handed over. Eagerly he broke the seal and opened it, to find that it consisted of two sheets of paper, covered with news from his daughter. To save space, and thus reduce the cost of delivery, Sarah's writing was small and cramped, as she squeezed all her letter onto the back of the sheet bearing the address and both sides of the second sheet. Isaac eagerly read its contents, which filled him with pleasure.

Later that evening, Isaac gathered the family around him and read the letter out loud.

"My Dear Family,

I hope that this letter finds you as well as it leaves me. I am now quite settled with the Wilmots and their children. I will tell you more of this later, but first will tell you of my journey to London.

It was a long and arduous journey and not very comfortable. The coachman drove the horses at a fast pace for most of the journey, which caused us much discomfort from the ruts and holes in the road. Along the way we stopped a number of times to pick up passengers and goods, which, for the most part were letters. Our first major stop was in the city of Ely, where we were able to get refreshment.

By the time we reached Cambridge, it was already quite dark, so I cannot say much about that fine city, except that it looked to be beautiful place, with many fine buildings. We had time for a meal, before we continued on our way. We would not reach London until after dawn the next day and I tried to sleep, without, I must confess, too much success.

Eventually we reached London and I was happy to find that the Wilmots had honoured the arrangements that had been made. A carriage was waiting to take me to their house and Mrs Wilmot was there to accompany me. Like you, dear mother, she is named Elizabeth. Our journey took us across the mighty River Thames by way of London Bridge. I was amazed at how busy it was, with ships and boats of all sizes along the banks and moving up and down the river. To now, I had thought our own Lynn to be a busy port, but this was far beyond anything I have seen there. Many of the craft were much larger than anything that has been seen on our river.

We continued on for some time into the County of Kent, until we reached the Wilmot's house. Again, I have to confess that this quite took away my breath. It is a large country house set in its own grounds, which in themselves seem to be as large as the whole of Lynn. As I have since discovered, it has many rooms, as well as a separate stables, where Mr Wilmot keeps a number of horses and several carriages.

Mr Wilmot is a very wealthy merchant and travels abroad a good deal. His house is filled with many wonderful things that he has brought back from these travels and I have determined to learn as much as I can about all these things, so that I can better instruct my young charges. In spite of his current wealth and position, Mr Wilmot came from humble origins and has acquired his present position through hard work. Up until now I have only met him on a couple of occasions, as he has been away tending his business, but he seems to be a kindly man with a pleasant disposition.

My two charges are both boys, James and Matthew, and are aged five and six years. Together, we occupy several rooms on the second floor of the house. They share a bedroom, whilst my room is next to it, in order to be at hand whenever I am needed. We also have another room we use as a schoolroom, filled with many books on a variety of subjects. We usually eat meals together here, or in another room next to it, where they can relax and play.

The Wilmots keep a number of servants to manage the house. I have to speak with the cook on a daily basis to discuss our food, which is then hauled up from the kitchens, which are in the basement of the house, to our floor, using a lift. One of the maids waits by the lift at the appointed time and fetches the meal to us. I almost feel like royalty, being attended in this manner.

When it is fine weather, I can take the boys out into the grounds of the house. How pleasant it is to sit in the shade of a tree with a book, while they play their games and enjoy fresh air and exercise.

You will be pleased to hear, my dearest father, that the Wilmot family are good church people. Each Sunday morning, we all go by carriage to the church in the local village. The vicar there is quite old and a very gentle man. His sermons are not so fiery as those that we hear in St Margaret's. Perhaps there are not so many sinners in these parts, that he has to reprove. After church, the whole family eat their meal together and the Wilmots spend the afternoon with their children, which gives me a little time to myself.

I am sorry if my letter is rather long and hope it does not cost too much to receive, but I wanted to tell you all how well I am doing and that I am happy in my new situation. I will write again when I am able, but perhaps not quite at such length next time.

Your loving daughter and sister, Sarah."

As William finished reading the letter, the children clapped their hands with delight, whilst Elizabeth dabbed at her eyes with a handkerchief. Isaac crossed over to her and placed his arm across her shoulder, at which she looked up. In spite of the moistness of her eyes, she was smiling.

Her daughter had found a good position and was obviously content, so she was happy as well.

Chapter Fourteen: New Friendships

In October 1760, the Leet Court was due to meet for the annual appointment of headboroughs and constables. Isaac and John Hart agreed to continue as headboroughs, but there was a new constable for the ward, Thomas Sharpe. This trio formed an effective partnership, that was to remain together for the next three years.

Thomas Sharpe was a carpenter and joiner. Isaac had had no direct dealings with him as a tradesman, but had met him on a few occasions socially. He found him a pleasant fellow and easy to get on with. Now that official duties brought them together more, they soon became firm friends.

In the March of 1761, Thomas invited Isaac and his family to join him after church one Sunday, at his house on Priory Lane. They would be celebrating one of Thomas's daughter's birthday. Isaac gladly accepted and the two families walked across to Thomas's house after morning service.

The house, on the side of the lane nearest the church, was slightly larger than the cottage that Isaac and Elizabeth had rented after their marriage, but not as spacious as their current tenement in Hampton Court.

Thomas's family consisted of his wife Sarah and two daughters, also Sarah, whose eleventh birthday it was that week, and Ann, who was seven and a half. As they chatted, Isaac found out that they had originally come from Suffolk. Thomas had been drawn to King's Lynn because, as a carpenter and joiner, he felt that there would be opportunities for him in the shipyards there. He had not been wrong, since, as well as maintaining his own workshop, he had been given plenty of work to do on new ships, where his carpentry skills were particularly called for in carving the various smaller fixtures and fittings that were needed. As someone who had come from outside of the town, however, Thomas was not a freeman of King's Lynn, but he had now lived there for around twelve years and both his daughters had been born there.

Whilst Sarah, Elizabeth and Judith chatted and put the finishing touches to the meal, Susanna and William joined the two Sharpe girls at play. Of course, young Sarah was the centre of attention, at least in her own eyes, for it was her birthday they were there to celebrate. As if often the case between siblings, she tended to argue quite a lot with her sister, Ann, and try to impose her will on the younger girl. As was evident over a number of visits, this was not uncommon. William, being the youngest in his family, was quite familiar with this pattern of behaviour and quickly developed a feeling of sympathy for Ann. He soon began to take her part and stick up for her, whilst Susanna tended to stay out of matters and leave it to the adults to mediate. William's defence of Ann surprised young Sarah and she stopped picking on her sister, at least while William was near. Ann herself was obviously pleased at this turn of events and quietly whispered in William's ear. "Thank you."

Later that day, once they had returned to Hampton Court, Isaac couldn't resist gently teasing William.

"Ah, son. I think you've got a friend there in Ann. She seems to like you."

His son muttered a few words and went up to the bedroom. Isaac smiled, as he saw that William had inherited his own habit of blushing at such comments.

They had had a good day, socialising with the Sharpe family and it was to be the first of many such days, as their friendship grew.

*   *   *   *   *

One such day spent together came in late March 1762, when news reached the town that a whale had been trapped and killed in Beverley Creek. The taking of the whale had occurred late on the Saturday, the 27th and the news reached most people when they attended morning service the next day. Beverley Creek was near the estuary of the River Ouse and about five miles from the centre of town. Thomas and Isaac agreed that this would be something that they all should see and Thomas made arrangements to borrow a horse and cart the next day. It was such a rare event that Isaac sent word to his employees that they might have the day off from work on the Monday and accompany them, if they wished.

There was an air of excitement the next morning, particularly amongst the younger children, as they all were ready soon after first light. Everyone was dressed in their warmest coats, as a precaution against the strong winds they were likely to encounter on the coast at this time of year. Elizabeth and Sarah had prepared baskets of food and drink to sustain them all during the day. Everyone clambered aboard the cart, including Isaac's two apprentices, Samuel and Edward, and, with Thomas at the reins, they moved off. Whilst this was a great adventure for the younger members of the group, it was also quite new to Isaac, who had rarely felt the need to leave the confines of the town.

The roads towards the coast were packed with others on a similar quest, some in carts like themselves, the more affluent with their own carriages, and a great number of others on foot. It would seem that King's Lynn was to be a quiet place that day, as most of its population was on its way to Beverley Creek.

After a little over an hour, they arrived at the site. The sight that greeted them was astonishing. Beverley Creek was one of many inlets on this part of the coast and it appeared that the whale had entered the creek and been unable to return to the sea. It now lay, beached on the bottom of the creek, having been dispatched by the crew of a whaler, who had been called from the town for this purpose. It had been fortunate to find such a crew still in port at this date, since all the rest of the whaling fleet had already set sail for the waters of Greenland, but this ship had been delayed by last minute repairs.

Hundreds of people were walking around the huge whale and Thomas decided that he would not be able to take the cart much closer, so they all disembarked. Samuel was left to stay with the horse, with the promise that he would be shortly relieved by Edward, whilst the remainder walked across the field towards the whale. Only when they came closer to it did they appreciate its size. It towered over them and its body at its broadest part was over twice the height of the tallest man. William, Ann and young Sarah all expressed their wonderment at such a beast. To them it seemed as big as a house and it very nearly was. It was later measured and found to be over fifty-six feet in length, with a girth of more than thirty-four feet.

At some point, all of them, including the children, had been alerted by the ringing of the bells of St Margaret's and had seen the whaling ships triumphantly return to port in July or August. They would berth in South Lynn, along the River Nar, where the main blubber houses were situated. By this time, their catch had been mainly stripped down into manageable lumps of blubber and meat, ready to be loaded onto carts and taken to the blubber house, where it would be rendered into the oil that would fuel thousands of lamps. For weeks, the area of South Lynn was subject to the appalling smell produced by this process, a fact Isaac remembered well from his time there. Whilst they had all seen the piles of huge bones lying on the decks of the whalers, this was the first time any in the party had seen an entire carcass.

"Just imagine our men having to do battle with something that size, to capture it on the high seas" commented Isaac, "Those tavern tales they tell are not as exaggerated as we thought."

Thomas murmured his assent. Whaling was a growing trade in the town and brought in a good income. So important was it that the sailors on the whalers were the only ones with protection from the naval press gangs and carried a certificate with them to prove it.

They strolled along the side of the whale for some time, in awe of its great size, before returning to the cart to eat the picnic they had brought with them. Afterwards, both the apprentices went off for another closer look at the whale, whilst children and parents discussed what they had seen. Eventually, about mid afternoon, they decided to return to town and set off on the journey back. As Thomas drove the cart, the rest of them looked back at the scene until they could no longer make out the whale.

The whale stayed by the creek for some days, whilst the mayor, on behalf of the town, disputed its ownership with the landowner, Nicholas Styleman, whose land adjoined the creek. Eventually the mayor prevailed and a number of men from the blubber houses were sent out to divide up the carcass and bring it back on carts for processing, producing a good windfall for the town coffers. As this was a sperm whale, the spermaceti wax could be extracted from the head and used to make candles. These were the most expensive type of candle and burnt with a bright, white light.

Chapter Fifteen: A Year of Change

Isaac was looking forward to 1763, with some excitement. In this year his only son, William, would be ready to start his apprenticeship. Early in the year, Isaac also took on another apprentice. This was at the request of the Corporation, who wished to place a boy from a poor family with him. This was Henry Mickleson. The corporation agreed to pay Isaac ten pounds from money left as a bequest for such purposes, known as Mr Horne's Charity. As Isaac himself had started his apprenticeship in a similar manner, he was pleased to be able to agree.

Isaac also decided that he would do everything possible to find a position for Judith and made sure that all his contacts amongst the merchants of the town were aware of this. This approach proved to be the right one, when he was told by John Hart of a kinsman of his, Joseph Hart in Cambridge, who had need of a governess. In the past two years, all the letters from Sarah, together with her occasional visits, had been very positive. It was clear that she had found a position very much to her liking and this, in turn, helped to persuade Judith (and her mother) that a similar career would suit her.

Arrangements were made with the family in Cambridge and, in the middle of March, the Forster family were once again awaiting the stage outside the *Duke's Head*. Judith was a naturally cheerful and optimistic young lady and was looking forward to her new life. Elizabeth was still tearful at seeing another daughter leave home, whilst Susanna and William welcomed the chance to be somewhere other than at their books. Isaac himself felt a sense of satisfaction at having found the position and hoped that Judith would take to it as well as had Sarah.

With the trunk loaded, it came time to say their farewells. William was the first to bid his sister good luck. When he was very young, William had had difficulty with pronouncing her name and ever since had used his own version, a habit that would stay with him all his life.

"Have a good journey, Juda. Do not forget to write. You know how we will enjoy all the news from Cambridge."

With that he gave her a hug and stepped back to allow his sister to say farewell. Isaac followed her and, as he had done before with Sarah, finished by pressing into her hand a small purse containing five sovereigns. Finally, it was Elizabeth's turn. She was determined not to show too much emotion, but she really couldn't help herself, holding her daughter tight, as if she would not let her go. When the coachman made the call for the passengers to board, Isaac placed a hand on Elizabeth's arm and gently urged her away. Judith clambered aboard the coach, which was soon on its way.

Judith did indeed send the promised letter and, once more, it gave Isaac great pleasure to know that a daughter of his was in a position that she found much to her satisfaction. She only had one child to look after at the moment, a girl of eight, who was the daughter of Joseph Hart, a prosperous corn merchant in the city. There was a much younger boy, of eighteen months, who would become her pupil at some time in the future. She really liked Cambridge. She wrote of a pleasant city, with many places to walk. She especially liked to stroll with her young charge along the banks of the river and gaze at the many fine buildings that made up the university.

Another area that she was enthusiastic about was in the centre of Cambridge, in the grounds of "the Mansion House", on the site of an old Augustinian priory. In the previous three years, great efforts had been made to establish a Botanical Gardens, covering about four acres, and complete with many glasshouses to grow rare specimens from warmer climes. Although the Gardens belonged to the University, Judith had, with the help of Mr Hart, who did a great deal of his trade with the University, obtained permission to visit the Gardens and had already become well acquainted with the Curator, Charles Miller. She spent much space in her letters describing all the rare and beautiful plants she was able to see on her visits.

Once again, Isaac and Elizabeth were content that another daughter had been settled into a good position.

*   *   *   *   *

Isaac and his family were regular churchgoers. Because of where they now lived, they usually attended services at St Margaret's, but, as it was where they grew up and were married, Isaac and Elizabeth always regarded All Saints as "their" church. Several times a year, mainly at the major festivals, they would make the journey to South Lynn to worship at All Saints. This would invariably be followed by a family meal at the *Eight Bells*.

In the spring of 1763, Isaac and the family were attending a service at St Margaret's, when they were shocked by an announcement made by the Reverend Bagge.

"I am sorry to have to tell you that the tower of All Saints church collapsed last night. We are not sure of the reason for this, but fortunately, no-one was injured. Please join me now in a prayer for our fellow worshippers at All Saints."

After the service, Isaac led the family across to South Lynn, to see the damage for themselves. The sight that greeted them made their hearts sink. The tower had been a square tower with battlements at the top. The tower itself had stood over eighty feet high, but this height had been extended another thirty feet by a pinnacle, topped by a weather vane. Now all the masonry lay on the ground by the main entrance to the church. Much of the fabric of the church around the west door appeared to have been severely damaged. Many of the local population had turned out and were now trying to clear away as much of the stone as was possible.

As they gazed on this scene of destruction, Elizabeth started to speak.

"Remember…"

This was all she said and, when Isaac turned to see why she had fallen silent, he saw that she was in tears. He put his arm around her shoulder and gently squeezed. She need say no more; he knew exactly what she meant. This place was so full of memories for them. To the left of the church stood the large tree where he had proposed to Elizabeth all those years ago. Then there had been the number of times they had attended services together there and walked back afterwards to the *Eight Bells*. As his gaze moved towards the doors of the church, he remembered the day, nearly twenty-four years since, when he had stood proudly on the steps of the church, his new bride on his arm. Now that spot was covered in fallen stones from the tower. The bells, that had rung out so joyously in recognition of their union, now lay among the rubble.

Yes, Isaac knew exactly what Elizabeth had meant. He turned again towards her and drew her close, before gently kissing her. Looking deep into her eyes, he knew that she recognised their shared sorrow at the damage to their church.

*   *   *   *   *

In April, Isaac received some bad news. His friend, Stephen Allen, had died after an illness lasting several months. Isaac was at his funeral on the 17th April, which was very well attended by the merchant class of the town. Stephen left a wife, Elizabeth, and three children, Mary, Stephen and Elizabeth, aged twelve, eight and one year old, respectively. With his income from the wine trade, as well as his inheritance from his father, Stephen was quite wealthy and owned considerable property in that part of town, including Hampton Court. His own house was quite a large one, directly opposite the main doors of St Margaret's Church. He left this to his daughter Mary, but it would remain in the hands of his widow until Mary reached twenty-one. Most of his property and his business were left in trust for young Stephen, whilst his wife received five thousand pounds immediately, and an income of a hundred pounds a year, whilst she remained a widow. Hampton Court was left to his youngest daughter, and he appointed trustees to look after it. These were both his brothers-in-law, George Hogge and Maxey Allen. The latter was the brother of Stephen's wife, whilst George Hogge belonged to one of the major merchant families in King's Lynn and was married to Stephen's sister, Mary. For some time he had been in a business partnership with Stephen and their combined fleet of ships traded, not only in wine, but also coal and other goods. For the foreseeable future, it would be one of these two, George Hogge or Maxey Allen, or their representatives, to whom Isaac would pay his quarterly rent.

Isaac felt quite sad at the death of Stephen. He had been a friend and companion for some time and, in spite of his own rise through the social strata of the town, Stephen had always remained so, with very few airs and graces. Isaac and Elizabeth had been frequent guests at the Allen's house, where they were introduced to the drinking of tea. Tea was an expensive drink, mainly due to the duty on it being set at that time at one hundred and nineteen percent. This made tea a real luxury at between six and ten pounds a pound. Those too poor to afford such prices could still indulge in the habit of tea drinking, however, either by resorting to buying smuggled tea, on which duty had not been paid, or by begging used tea leaves from the houses of the rich. The housekeepers at these houses were known to make a supplement to their incomes in this way.

The Allen's tea had been neither smuggled nor used before, but was the proper article. It was kept in a caddy, a small chest, which was normally kept locked. In the caddy, it was normal to have two types of tea. One would be a stronger type of tea, such as the green "gunpowder" variety, or black Pekoe, whilst the other would be a milder variety, the most popular of which was congou. A blend of the two was made to the taste of the host and the resultant drink was served with sugar. Isaac had taken to this drink so much that, in a particularly prosperous period for the loft, he had acquired his own caddy and tea, for special occasions.

Of course, the Allen's also had a good wine cellar, a benefit of being in the trade, and had shared examples from this with Isaac and Elizabeth on a number of occasions.

*　　*　　*　　*　　*

With Judith's future seeming secure, Isaac could now turn his attention to his other children, especially William. William had made good progress with his studies and Isaac had received excellent reports from the Free School. In February, William had celebrated his thirteenth birthday and, by the end of June, Isaac considered him ready to leave school and enter the sail loft as an apprentice. Of course, William knew everyone in the loft and had already spent many hours there after lessons, helping out where he could with some of the menial tasks, like helping the two apprentices bring canvas and rope to where Isaac and Thomas Tilson needed them.

Isaac was determined not to show any favouritism towards his son. He would be expected to work hard and, if anything, Isaac would be more critical of any poor work on his part, than he would be to the other apprentices. Most of the fetching and carrying, keeping the loft clean and tidy, making deliveries, and other tasks that were not so popular, would be shared between William and Edward, whilst Samuel, who would complete his apprenticeship later in the year, was treated now as a qualified sail-maker, entrusted to work unsupervised for long periods. Or that was the impression he was given, for Isaac kept a careful eye on all who worked for him. He had been taught high standards by his own master and was determined to maintain them now in his loft.

Isaac believed that his apprentices should understand how their handiwork was going to be used and should be familiar with the various terms used when referring to sails and their associated equipment on board ship. Quite early in William's apprenticeship, as he had done for all his previous apprentices, Isaac took his son to the quayside. There he found the ship mastered by Henry Crow, his long-time neighbour. Father and son went aboard and soon found the master mariner, who was with another familiar face, his son and formerly Isaac's apprentice, the younger Henry. The two older men greeted each other enthusiastically. Of course, William was also quite familiar with the Crows, having met them often in Hampton Court. He politely doffed his hat, slightly inclining his head forward as he did so.

"So then," began Henry senior, "Young William has started to learn the trade and you want us to show him something about our sails."

Isaac agreed. "Thank you, Henry. I hope it doesn't inconvenience you."

"Not at all. I'm going to leave it to young Henry here to explain things. After all, he knows better than I do what you expect William to learn. In the meantime, perhaps you'd care to come to my cabin for some conversation and some wine I picked up on my last voyage. We can also discuss some repairs and replacements I need."

With that the two fathers wandered away, leaving the sons to begin their tour.

After exchanging a few pleasantries, Henry began to speak about the boat and, in particular, the sails.

"Very well," he began, "This ship is called the *Success* and is a three-masted barque. The long pieces of wood attached to the masts are the yards and we hang the sails from those. Because most of the yards are positioned across the width of the ship, we say that the sails on those yards are square-rigged. Some of our sails, however, are set basically along the line of the keel, so those are said to be fore-and-aft rigged. Is that clear to you?"

"Yes, I've come across those terms before. Please go on."

"Fine. Now, on the *Success* we normally have up to four sails on the centre mast, which is the main mast. At the bottom is the main-course, or main-sail. On the yard above that, we have the main topsail and then, above that the main top-gallant. Because we have quite a tall mast, we can set another sail above the top-gallant, which called the main-royal. This is usually only used in good weather, though. Some larger ships have further sails, known as sky-sails or even, on very tall masts, a moon-sail, or stargazer. Can you remember the sails we have here?"

"I think so," said William, "Main-course, main-topsail, main top-gallant and main-royal."

"Very good. You've got a good memory. It took me a long time to get all the names right, and I'd been to sea a few times before I started with your father. Let's go on.

"The mast in front of the main mast is the fore mast and the names of the sails follow the same pattern. There's the foresail, or fore-course, the fore-topsail, fore-top-gallant and fore-royal. Larger ships can have even more, like sky-sails and moon-sails. The mast at the rear is the mizzen-mast and, on this ship, the sails here are different shapes and fore-and-aft rigged. The lower one, which we call the driver, or sometimes simply the mizzen, is suspended from and stretched along, a boom known as a gaff. It's a four sided sail, but the top edge rises up with the boom, whilst the foot drops slightly, on another boom. Trust me, it's an awkward shape to cut out and then sew together. Above that is a shoulder-of-mutton sail, which is a triangle and is attached to the mast. Are you still following me?"

"Oh, yes. I'd like to see the *Success* when she puts to sea, with all these sails set."

"Oh, you're not likely to see them all set close to shore. It would make it hard to manage. Still, who knows, perhaps old Isaac will let you come for a trip with us some time, when you could find us under full sail.

"Anyway, those are the main sails we use, but there are lot of others we also use. See all the ropes attached to the masts and going to the bow or stern of the barque?" William nodded. "Those are called stays and we can hang a number of stay-sails from them to give us extra speed. We can use quite a few of these stay-sails. Nearly all these stay-sails are triangular in shape. Probably the most important of these stay-sails is the one nearest the bow of the ship, called a jib. The jib is set as far forward as possible, with the stay being attached to the bowsprit. That's the bit that sticks out out the very front of the barque."

The tour of the *Success* continued for some time, with Henry showing William to all parts of the vessel and continuing his explanation. Whilst at times it seemed like Henry was speaking a foreign language, with all the different names for the sails and their rigging, it was very useful to hear from someone who had trained as a sail-maker and who was now relying on sails to help him earn a living. Henry could explain what the sailor expected from the sail and how the high standards set by Isaac were really important.

Eventually, Isaac and the elder Henry reappeared, having concluded their business. It had obviously gone well, as Isaac was in a good mood. He told William that he could stay a little longer with young Henry.

"Not too long, though. I expect to see you back at the loft in good time to tidy up at the end of the day. And thank you, young Henry, for your help today. If you ever decide to settle down on shore again, I'm sure there will always be a job for you at my loft."

"Thank you, sir" said Henry, respectfully.

With that Isaac bade farewell to the barque's Master and made his way ashore along the gang-plank. William knew better than to take too much advantage of Isaac's good mood and only stayed a short while longer, before he himself went ashore and walked the short distance to the loft. He had enjoyed his time with Henry and felt that it had been a really useful day.

*   *   *   *   *

Towards the end of 1763, Isaac began the last year in which he would serve as headborough. Whilst John Hart continued to serve as the other headborough for the ward, Thomas Sharpe decided to step down as constable and his place was taken by Robert Haycock. Haycock was a huge man, who by trade was a smith. He specialised in the metal fittings for ships, particularly anchors. Although Isaac knew him to be essentially a gentle giant, who would not seek out or cause trouble, he also knew that his sheer physical presence and obvious strength would be a powerful deterrent, should any sort of trouble arise.

Haycock's main employers were the Bagge family, whose ships were also amongst Isaac's customers. The Bagges were one of the oldest and most successful dynasties in the town. Originally landowners, they had come to King's Lynn and founded the brewery that bore their name. Since then, they had expended their interests into many other areas, including shipping. Two public houses, the *Woolpack* and the *Red Cow*, plus a lot of property in the centre of town, were also part of their domain. William Bagge had run this business empire for some years, but had died the previous year and the business had become a common venture between his two sons, William and Thomas.

Chapter Sixteen: The End of an Era

William's education as a sail-maker continued apace. Although Henry Mickleson had started a few months before him, he strove to match him at every stage. Isaac was pleased with the competition between the two apprentices, as he knew that they would develop faster and become useful additions to the loft. Now that Samuel Browne had completed his apprenticeship, Isaac had two time-served sail-makers, in Samuel and Thomas Tilson, and three apprentices to assist him in the loft. When Isaac had started his apprenticeship, William Elstobb had been the main sail-maker in town, but now there were several lofts in different parts of King's Lynn. Isaac's loft, however, had a good reputation and the various contacts he had made with ships' masters and their owners meant that he was always busy and could afford to maintain the loft, even employing other journeymen sail-makers from time to time.

The apprentices basically learnt by watching a task being performed, before attempting to emulate it, usually on a spare piece of canvas. One they had mastered a particular skill, they might be allowed to work on an actual sail, under supervision. All the time, they were learning the language of the craft. They learnt to refer to the top of a square sail as the head, whilst the bottom was called the foot. The sides of the sails were the leeches. The seams at the sides were reinforced by sewing in ropes, called bolt-ropes. The bottom corners of the sail were known as clues. Here, William's education proved, indirectly, to be a great help. He had had to learn many different things, usually by rote, during his time at the grammar school and, if he wished to avoid the anger of the schoolmaster, and possible punishment, he had had to develop a facility for remembering facts. He was, therefore, quicker that Henry to assimilate all the new terminology.

Isaac was sitting at his desk one day, sorting out his accounts and deciding what new stock of raw materials would be needed, when paused for a moment to watch the activity in the loft. Samuel and Edward were working on the seams of a sail, which was draped across the floor of the loft, The seams had first been folded and, since this was to be a mainsail and would need to billow out in the wind, the seams were wider at the head and foot than in the middle of the sail. Then they would be sewn twice, working from the foot to the head. This stitching would need to be strong, to withstand the forces that would act on the sail in a strong wind, so there were between one hundred and twenty-four and one hundred and forty-four stitches per yard of seam. Isaac, not wishing to receive complaints from any master mariners, preferred the higher figure.

On the other side of the loft, Thomas was working on the other half of the sail, which was more complete. He was showing William and Henry how to form eyelets in the sail. He would cut a hole in the canvas and then stretch and shape it, using a fid, which was a long conical tool made from wood or whalebone. Once the eyelet was made to the correct size that was required for its particular purpose, the edges were reinforced with a grommet. This was made from a strand of rope, laid round the hole three times and then sewn into place with rope twine. Once more, there was a long list of names for the various sizes of eyelets and there purposes. William and Henry's heads swum with talk of cringles, bunt-lines, reefs, garnets, etc. Whilst they might feel that they were having a struggle to learn all the skills of the sail-maker's craft, Isaac, with his long experience, could see the progress being made and was pleased with what he saw. He could be hard on his apprentices at times, when they did not match his high standards, but he was also ready to give them encouragement and a few words of praise, when he saw that they were trying hard.

All the skills needed to be practised many times. As well as learning to sew the sail itself, the apprentices needed to be skilled in all the additional fittings that went to make up the complete sail. William had, for example, spent hours mastering the art of splicing ropes, particularly splicing pieces onto the bolt-lines and then forming them into a loop, into which a metal piece could be included. On board ship, these loops offered a way of securing the sails.

As his apprentices progressed, he also made sure that they understood the business side of the loft. One day they might set up for themselves and would need to be able to cope with this. They needed to be able to calculate the amount of canvas needed for a new sail. Working from the overall dimensions and shape of the sail, whilst making allowances for the various seams, they had to work out how many strips of cloth would be needed and how much this would cost. Then they had to add in the costs of linings and bolt-ropes, and all the other fittings. Add to this the time taken to make the sail and they should be able to arrive at a selling price, to make a reasonable profit. At first, Isaac would make his apprentices work out all of this from scratch. Only once he felt they had understood the processes involved would he show them the books of tables he had, which had already done these calculations for the most common types of sails. Of course, not every apprentice could cope with this side of the business and Isaac could soon form an idea of which ones would go on to be masters in their own right and which would remain as sail-makers, working for other people.

William did have a good head for the business side of things and Isaac felt satisfied that the loft would be in safe hands when it came time for him to hand over the reins. Indeed, William found the business side more interesting than the process of actually making sails. Whilst he was anxious to please his father and worked hard at everything, he often wondered if he would want to spend the rest of his life cooped up in a dimly lit sail loft. But, for now, this was the trade that he was learning and he made every effort to master it fully.

$$* \quad * \quad * \quad * \quad *$$

The next problem which Isaac needed to address would be Susanna's future. Unlike her sisters, Susanna had not shown any aptitude in academic studies and would not be following them as a teacher or governess. But she was now of an age where she needed to find a position in life and become independent. Whilst she may not have shone in her school studies, she was always a very practical type and cheerfully helped Elizabeth around their home with all the daily chores.

This cheerful and practical nature gave Isaac an idea of how she would best be suited. Once more, he began to sound out his various contacts. The answer he wanted came from a familiar source, Elizabeth Allen, the widow of his old friend, Stephen. She had need of a personal maid and, knowing Susanna, would be happy to take her on. And so Susanna made the short move from Hampton Court to the large house opposite the church to begin a new life in service. She was very happy with this. She was sure that she would be able to cope with the job and, when she had any free time, was very close to her family. Not for her a long coach journey to another part of the country.

*   *   *   *   *

Isaac tried to visit his old master as often as he could. The old man was now nearly ninety-five years old. Long hours working in the dull light of a sail loft had taken its toll and he was now nearly blind. His hearing was also failing and it was often necessary to speak loudly and repeat things several times. He did, however, remain in a reasonably good physical shape and would enjoy a walk with Isaac to the shore-line, where he could feel the sun and the wind on his face. Occasionally, he could make out the vague shape of a ship, as it sailed on the river, and would guess as to its type from its size and the set of its sails. More often than not, he was right; as far as Isaac would tell him, he was always right. He no longer was able to read, even with the aid of a magnifying glass, but he could still remember the words of some of his favourite poems and would take great pleasure in reciting them.

As summer turned to autumn in 1765, the weather worsened and Isaac and his master could not walk so often together. The lack of fresh air and exercise had a bad effect on old William, as he seemed, all of a sudden, to lose a lot of his strength. Whilst he still enjoyed long conversations with his former apprentice, he now rarely left his chair. Isaac worried that he was not feeding himself well. He made sure that he always had some food in the house and knew that he was being supported by local charities and by the Quakers. He also had good neighbours, who took turns in cooking for him. Nevertheless, Isaac could see that his overall condition was worsening and feared the effects of a harsh winter.

William did survive the winter, however, and, as the days lengthened, began to speak to Isaac about resuming their walks. After the high winds that were common in March had subsided, and April brought better weather, he asked Isaac if they could venture out for a walk. Although they left the house and started along the lane outside, it soon became apparent that a walk to the riverside would be out of the question. William was far too weak. Instead, Isaac assisted him back to his door and then fetched his chair outside, so he could at least enjoy the sun, until it began to set across the far side of the river.

A few days later, Isaac had a visitor at the loft. It was the younger William Elstobb. His visit was out of the ordinary, but for Isaac it was half-expected. He could tell at once from his demeanour that he bore sad news. Isaac was at his desk, writing a bill of sale, but immediately put down his quill, rose from his seat, and came round the desk to where William stood.

"I'm sorry, Isaac, but I have to tell you that my father passed away last night. He was found this morning, sitting in his chair, by one of the neighbours."

Isaac paused for a moment to take in this sad news, before he replied.

"William, I'm so sorry to hear that. I know that you must be devastated." He extended his right hand, which was taken by William, and then put his other hand, in a gesture of sympathy, on the other man's shoulder.

"Thank you, Isaac. I know how much he meant to you also. You are part of our family. We can take some consolation from the fact that he lived a long and good life, and that his end was peaceful"

"Indeed. What happens now?"

"I have spoken to one of the Quaker elders and the funeral and burial will take place on the twenty-sixth of the month. I know I can count on you to help carry the coffin."

"Of course. And all my loft will be there. After all, this would not be here, were it not for all that he taught me, all those years ago."

"Thank you again, Isaac. I'm sorry to be the bearer of such news. We will meet again at the funeral."

With that, the two men said their farewells and William departed, no doubt to impart the news to the many others in the town for whom his father had been a friend and an example.

*   *   *   *   *

On the appointed day, the funeral service for William Elstobb, master sail-maker, was held in the Friends' Meeting House. The coffin was carried in on the shoulders of Isaac, William Elstobb junior, Daniel Locust, Thomas Burch, Thomas Tilson and Samuel Browne, and placed on the trestles at the front of the seating. For the fourth time in his life, Isaac was to experience a Quaker service. On this occasion, the room was crowded. Old William had led a long life, made many friends, and touched so many lives. Now, whether Quakers or not, they had come to pay their respects.

As with the previous services, members of the congregation rose and said whatever they felt was appropriate. Many of those present were moved to do just that, speaking of his contribution to town life, to the Quakers, and his work as a master craftsman. The tributes continued for a long time.

Isaac and William had agreed that they would wait until the end of the meeting, before having their say, with William speaking last of all. William had discussed this with the elders and they had agreed. As the flow of tributes from the meeting began to slow, William looked across at Isaac and nodded. Isaac rose to his feet.

"Friends," he began "I feel I can call you all friends. After all, we are in the Meeting House of the Society of Friends. Many of you know me and I certainly can see many friends here today. For those who may not know me, I am Isaac Forster and I was taught to be a sail-maker by

William Elstobb. He took me into his house, when I was fourteen, and agreed to have me as an apprentice. Before that, I was in the care of the parish. William and Margaret, God rest her soul, became like parents to me, whilst their sons, William here and Nicholas, God rest his soul, were like brothers to me. After I finished my apprenticeship, I stayed on with him for a few years, before, with a lot of help and encouragement from my master, I set up in business on my own.

"Since then, he remained my friend and was always happy to give me advice and help. As a master, he set high standards, which I try to pass on to my own apprentices. But he could be helpful in other ways. He certainly had a hand in my getting together with, and eventually marrying, my dear wife Elizabeth.

"I will always remember William Elstobb. He was a master, but also a father figure to me. He was an inspiration to me throughout my life. But above all, he was a friend. Those of you that have been on the wrong end of a reprimand for work that was not up to standard, or at least his high standards, may be surprised to know that he had a softer side. Both he and Margaret loved poetry and would read it together often, so I would like to read you a short piece of one of his favourite poems, which is, fittingly, on the subject of Friendship."

Isaac pulled from the pocket of his coat the book of Isaac Thompson's poetry, that William and Margaret had bought over thirty-five years before. He opened it at a page he had marked before and began to read

"Yet some remain, (alas the Number's few!)
Whose steady Feet, that ancient Path pursue;
Smit with the noble Love of V i r t u e, those
Dare yet be Friends, tho' half the World are Foes.
Such Souls are they which strict Alliance claim,
Meet Heart with Heart, and mingle Flame with Flame.
Together, these a boundless Flight can take,
Yet such a Flight as Truth itself may make.
For no romantick Strain here swells the Mind,
But all is real, artless, undesign'd;
The Tongue unskil'd in Compliments to flow,

Where Substance is possess'd, no need of show.
Thrice happy Breasts are those, which thus maintain
True Friendship's Laws, and wear the lib'ral Chain!
The sordid Soul may grovel on below,
And feel no Joys, but those the Senses know;
The Great, in Pomp, may vainly swell with Pride,
True Friends are happier than the World beside;
When each his Breast with mutual Freedom tells,
Nor Fault nor Virtue from his Friend conceals ;
Each Joy, or anxious Care, in ev'ry State,
Delights them both, or both divide the Weight,
For both together stand oppos'd to Fate."

Isaac finished, closed the book and sat down. A silence fell upon the meeting, which seemed to last an eternity, before William stood up, to start the final oration.

"Thank you, Isaac. I think you have said in those words what everyone is thinking." A murmur of assent came from the congregation.

"My father had a long life, and, while the latter years may not always have kind to him, he remained in good temper and cheerful disposition until the end. He was my father, but, like Isaac, I also found him to be my friend. Like any father, he had hopes that I would follow him into the sail-making business, but, when I decided on another path, he did not stand in my way. Instead, he helped me as much as he could and encouraged my ambition. It fell to my late brother Nicholas, God rest his soul, to take over the business, and now I feel that William's legacy lies firmly on the shoulders of Isaac. I don't think that my father could be better served. And, we must remember, that he died knowing this to be the case. I am sure, from talking to him, that he was content that this was so.

"Goodbye, dear father, may your soul rest in the peace you deserve."

William sat down. After a minute or so, the elders rose and started to shake hands with each other, indicating that the service was at an end. The six pallbearers took up the coffin and took it out through the doors. They carried it all the way to the burial ground, where old William was laid to rest, alongside his wife and younger son.

As they were leaving the burial ground, Isaac took the book of poems from his pocket and went to give it to William.

"No, Isaac." William said softly, "Please keep it and when you read it, remember my father."

Isaac muttered his thanks, then turned away, the tears welling up in his eyes. This was truly the end of an era.

Chapter Seventeen: Swordbearer

The later months of 1766 and early 1767 saw a number of changes in the sail loft. Edward Barrett completed his apprenticeship in October of 1766. At around the same time, John Jenkins reappeared in the town, having decided to remain ashore. Isaac noticed that he spent a lot of time socialising with both Edward Barrett and Thomas Tilson. They were often to be seen together in the *Prince of Wales*, drinking and having quite earnest discussions. It did come as a bit of a surprise, however, when they asked Isaac to join them one day. Isaac wondered if John was seeking work with him and wondered how he could let him down gently. The size of his payroll was already a bit more than he would have liked, even though they were kept busy with work. He decided, however, to go along and listen to what would be said.

Once they were settled with some drinks, John started to speak.

"Mr Forster..." he began.

"Please, John, we've known each other a long time now and I'm no longer your master. It's Isaac to all of you."

"Very well, er, Isaac," continued his former apprentice, "As you know, I've decided to leave the sea and come ashore. I've done fairly well for myself and have travelled a lot. As a result, I've made a number of contacts, particularly in London. Now I've found an opportunity to open my own sail loft there."

Isaac felt a slight sense of relief. He would not have to turn down his former apprentice.

"Well done, John. I wish you every success in this venture."

"Ah, yes. Thank you, Isaac, but this not the whole story. You see, I need some help there and have asked Edward and Thomas here if they would like to join me. I know that they must be excellent at their craft, if you've been the one to teach them. They've both expressed an interest, but we all wanted to speak to you first."

Now Isaac felt a bit shocked. Rather than expanding his work-force, he would now be losing two good men. But, of course, he would be powerless to stop them, if they had made up their minds to go. After spending a short time digesting the news he had just received, Isaac spoke.

"John, Thomas, Edward. I appreciate it that you've told me of your intentions and I'd not stand in your way, even if I could. You can go with my blessing. It seems I will need to look out for at least one more sail-maker to help fill the gap that you'll leave."

It was Thomas who then intervened. "Look, nothing's going to happen this side of the New Year, so we're not going to leave straight away. Perhaps you'll be able to find somebody before business picks up again in the spring."

"Yes, of course," replied Isaac, "Well, let us toast your new business and wish it every success."

With that, Isaac ordered more beer for them all and they spent a merry evening, talking about the future, remembering old times and toasting each other until quite late.

As it happened, Isaac need not have worried about being left short-handed. In the New Year, Henry Crow the younger called at the loft to tell Isaac that he too had had enough of life at sea. Henry had married just three years after completing his apprenticeship and, whilst he had enjoyed his life at sea, now felt that he wanted to spend more time with his family. Having heard that there might be a place vacant at the loft, he had decided that this might be a good time to settle down. Isaac remembered the conversation he had had a few years back, on the deck of the *Success*, when he had virtually promised Henry a job. Now he had the chance to make good on that promise and welcomed his former apprentice back into the loft.

With Samuel Browne and Henry Crow to assist him, as well as his apprentices, Isaac felt that a good balance had been restored to the loft. He would always be able to find journey-men to cope with surges in demand.

*   *   *   *   *

A General Election was to be held in 1768 and this was causing great commotion in the town, as, for the first time since 1747, it was to be contested. The reasons for this, which also affected many other parts of the country, could be traced back to events of several years before.

John Wilkes was a radical Member of Parliament, who, in 1762, was vehemently opposed to the new Prime Minister, John Stuart, 3rd Earl of Bute. He expressed his feelings through a weekly newspaper he founded, *The North Briton*. Even the title was an indirect attack on Bute, who had his own newspaper, called *The Briton*. One of the main causes of Wilkes' anger concerned the peace terms, agreed to by Bute, at the end of the Seven Years War, which Wilkes considered too generous to France. When George III, at the Opening of Parliament in 1763, gave a speech, generally supposed to be written by Bute, praising the Treaty of Paris, Wilkes turned his fire on the king, in issue 45 of his paper. Forty-five was a not insignificant number, following the Jacobite uprising of 1745. This angered the king so much that he had general warrants issued for the arrest of Wilkes and his publishers. A total of forty-nine people were arrested under these warrants. At the later hearing, Wilkes argued that the use of general, rather than specific, warrants was unconstitutional. He also claimed parliamentary privilege in answer to the charge of libel against him and the Lord Chief Justice, Lord Camden, agreed with him and, in his address to the jurors, said, "This warrant is unconstitutional, illegal, and absolutely void. It is a general warrant, directed to four messengers to take up any person, without naming or describing them, together with their papers." Wilkes was freed and allowed to resume his place as a member of parliament.

The case had received national notoriety, with people in the streets chanting the slogan "Wilkes, Liberty and number Forty-five", in reference to the edition of the paper. Ever since, the argument had raged concerning the use of general warrants to arrest people. The King and many of his ministers believed them to be a good thing and particularly useful in stifling dissent, whilst others saw them as a weakening of the principles and liberties that had been won by the Glorious Revolution of 1688. It was to be this question of general warrants that would dominate the 1768 campaign.

Two of the three candidates for the Lynn seat had a familiar ring to them. Firstly, there was a Walpole. This was not, however, the Horatio Walpole elected in 1747. He had been elevated to the House of Lords in 1757 on the death of his father and was now Baron Walpole of Wolterton. He had been succeeded as a member for Lynn by his cousin, Horace Walpole. However, in 1767, Horace had sent a letter to the Mayor, announcing his intention to retire from parliament. In his place stood Thomas Walpole, the brother of the former M.P., Horatio. Once more the taverns of King's Lynn would resound to the campaign song of the Walpoles.

Come fill up a bumper, and round let us stand;
Old England's our toast, take your glasses in hand –
May loyalty, liberty, flourish in Lynn,
And a Walpole, a Walpole, for ever be in.
Hearts of oak are we still and true honest men,
We always are ready,
Steady, boys, steady,
And a Walpole, a Walpole, shall ever be in!

The other familiar candidate was Sir John Turner, who had remained unopposed since 1747. Both he and Walpole were known to be in favour of general warrants.

But there was also to be another candidate. At the Mayor's Feast on September 29th 1766, the High Sheriff of the County of Norfolk, Crisp Molineux, announced that he would be a candidate in the next General Election, whenever that might be. He was against the use of general warrants and thus his target was Sir John.

Everyone knew that an election was in the offing, not least the Corporation. In 1766, there had been only five men qualified as freemen of the town and thus eligible to vote, but, in the following year, there were twenty-three. This was followed in the months leading up to the election by another nineteen. Many of these freedoms were gained by purchase, rather than the usual routes of completing an apprenticeship or by patrimony. Others were granted to people who had qualified many years before, but, for whatever reason, had not applied for their freedom until now, their memories having been jogged by interested parties. However, when it was later seen how these newly enfranchised freemen voted, neither side had made a significant gain through these extra votes. Many, if not all, of the three hundred or so eligible voters were approached with various inducements to sway their votes. Where a freeman had moved elsewhere in the country, like Isaac's former apprentices, John, Thomas and Edward, there would be offers of transport and hospitality to ensure that they returned for the election. And, as was usual, virtually every inhabitant of the town, man, woman or child, whether a voter or not, had an opinion and was willing to campaign vigorously for their preferred candidate, by whatever means they saw fit. With all the ale and hospitality on offer, everyone considered the election a splendid form of entertainment.

One who did not join in with this bout of election fever was Isaac. Although he had firm views about where his votes would be placed and attended a few gatherings to hear the candidates' speeches, he stayed clear of the taverns, where the beer flowed freely, courtesy of the prospective members of parliament. He still remembered 1747 and how poor Nicholas's state of health had been affected by such excesses. And, of course, he recalled the fate of John Harvey. Over twenty years later, he did not wish to become embroiled in the rough and tumble of the election.

Although a large number of voters pledged their votes to Crisp Molineux and said that he would be their only choice, he urged his supporters to also vote for Thomas Walpole. His thinking was that Walpole would be elected in any case and that the real fight was for second place. Feeling that this would give him the best chance, he thus encouraged his supporters to boost Walpole's vote, even though their political ideas were not closely aligned. Isaac was of a mind to follow this advice and would duly cast his votes for Walpole and Molineux.

The election took place on Monday March 21st 1768, with the usual crowds filling the Tuesday Market Place to watch the three hundred and twelve freemen arrive to cast their votes. Isaac left it late in the day to vote, having spent most of the day in the loft, taking advantage of the relative quiet to catch up with paperwork. He walked up to the hustings, meeting along the way Daniel Locust, who had been similarly occupied with business matters, and they cast their votes at around the same time. As it was so late in the proceedings, they decided to stay and see how things turned out. The last two people to vote were Charles Turner, the Mayor, and his brother, Sir John, the candidate. Once everyone else had voted, they had been called from out of the *Duke's Head*, just before the polls closed.

The poll clerks had been keeping a running tally of the votes, with each of around thirty pages being checked and totalled as the day progressed, so it was only a short delay before Charles Turner, as the returning officer, announced the result to the crowds in the square. As many expected, Thomas Walpole led with 200 votes. After the cheers had died down sufficiently for the Mayor to be heard, second place was announced and Charles Turner was obviously pleased to confirm that his brother had polled 174 votes and thus become the second Member of Parliament for King's Lynn. This produced even more cheering, particularly from the large group standing outside the *Duke's Head*, enjoying Sir John's generosity. It took a while before Molineux's total of 159 votes could be announced, but even then very few of the crowd actually heard the figure, while most did not really care.

"Well," said Daniel to Isaac, as they walked away, "It looks like Sir John's bought himself a few more years in parliament."

"Indeed so." concurred Isaac.

This speculation on the part of the two sail-makers was not wide of the mark. It was later estimated that Sir John had again spent around two thousand pounds, in bribes and hospitality, to influence the result.

It was also clear after the vote that Molineux's tactic of asking his voters to support Walpole as well was a bad mistake. Confident of victory, Walpole had not spent much time canvassing for support and, on election day, could only count on seven voters to "plump" for him and, even then, only four actually did. For the rest, he would have to rely on the second votes of the other candidates. A hundred of Molineux's supporters, including Isaac, acceded to his request to give their second votes to Walpole. Without these, Walpole would have come third in the poll and the line of Walpoles representing the town, which stretched back to the Restoration of Charles II, would have been broken.

*   *   *   *   *

Two days after the election, Isaac and Elizabeth went to a funeral in St Margaret's Church. The funeral was that of Giles Beeton. He had not been a close friend of Isaac's, but Isaac felt he had to go because he had been the brother-in-law of Thomas Burch, having been married to Thomas's sister, Sarah.

When Thomas told him of the death, Isaac had expressed surprise.

"But surely," he had said, "he was not that old. What caused his death?"

"You're right, Isaac. He was only forty eight years of age. I'm afraid he was, in a way, a victim of the election campaign."

Thomas went on to explain that Giles Beeton had been a strong supporter of Sir John Turner. He had attended most of the meetings and spent a lot of time trying to persuade fellow voters to vote for Sir John. At one of these meetings, he had over-indulged in the refreshments supplied by the candidate and was quite inebriated when he left to go home for the night. His own house was a fair distance from the *Duke's Head*, where the meeting had been held, and he had come by pony and trap. Apparently, he managed to reach his house, whether by his own skills in driving the trap, or the pony's instincts, but then, in descending from the trap, had stumbled and fallen forward, knocking into the rear of the pony. This had startled the animal, causing it to kick out with its rear legs. Giles had been caught a severe blow to his head and, when his wife, Sarah, hearing the commotion, had come out and discovered him, he was unconscious and bleeding profusely. He did not recover consciousness and died the next morning.

Isaac had expressed his sympathy and promised Thomas that he would attend the funeral, to support Thomas and his sister, who was now left with four young children, two boys and two girls, whose ages ranged from five to twelve years old. Isaac had met Giles on a number of occasions, particularly when he was a headborough. Giles Beeton was a merchant, dealing mainly in corn and flour, and, although not from one of the major families that dominated the Corporation of the town, had been called upon to act as one of three affeerors for the Leet Court. He had served in this capacity for several years and then had become Swordbearer for the town. It was not a surprise, therefore, to find the Mayor, and most of the Aldermen and Councillors at his funeral.

Afterwards, Thomas and his sister both thanked Isaac and Elizabeth for their presence. Isaac commented on the large turnout, to which Sarah replied, "Yes, I'm pleased that his service to the town seems to have been appreciated. It also showed how many other people's lives were touched by Giles."

*   *   *   *   *

Whilst Sarah and Judith did not visit their parents often, they were both good letter writers and Isaac and Elizabeth looked forward to these letters. Usually they were fairly ordinary, detailing their life with the families they served, but in late November came a letter from Judith that was far from ordinary. Isaac had read it when it was delivered and left the loft immediately, to share its contents with Elizabeth.

"My Dear Family. I hope you continue in good health. I shall be coming home at Christmas to see you all, but I simply couldn't wait 'til then to share my news with you.

In my walks in the Gardens, of which I have often told you, I have encountered a most pleasant man, named Thomas Randale. He shares my love of plants and many other things besides. I have had some acquaintance with him previously, as he helps his father run the local livery stable, which the family often use.

In short, he would like to meet you all, especially you, dear father. He will travel to King's Lynn with me and hopes to stay a few days. Perhaps accommodation could be arranged for him at this time.

I look forward to seeing you all soon.

Your ever loving daughter and sister, Judith"

As Isaac finished reading the letter, he and Elizabeth exchanged glances. For several moments, nothing was said, before Elizabeth broke the silence.

"Isaac, do you think…?"

There was no need for her to finish the question. As usual, they were both thinking along the same lines. Isaac nodded.

"Yes, I do." He could read the message between the lines. "I think our daughter has found someone she is ready to love. And who knows where that might lead? Let us look forward to meeting this Thomas Randale and let us hope that he is right for Judith."

Two days before Christmas, Isaac, Elizabeth and William were outside the *Duke's Head* to meet the Cambridge stage. The first person to alight from the stage was a tall, well built man in his mid-twenties. On reaching the ground, he turned and offered his hand to assist the next passenger to descend from the coach. It was Judith, who immediately hurried across to greet her family. Then she turned to the man, who was standing, somewhat nervously, a few feet away.

"Mother, father, this is Thomas."

Isaac, Elizabeth and William all greeted Thomas Randale warmly. Then the luggage was loaded on to a handcart and the family set off for Hampton Court. Elizabeth had insisted that Thomas would take all his meals with the family, whilst Isaac had found him a room at the *Prince of Wales*. But first there would be time to find out more about this young man who had now become part of Judith's life.

As Judith had already told them in her letters, Thomas worked alongside his father in the livery stables that was the family business. He was twenty-five years old, just a year older than Judith herself. Elizabeth was curious to know more about how they had met.

"Well, I suppose it had a little to do with the family business," replied Thomas, smiling, "We had an arrangement with the Botanical Gardens, whereby we would supply them with horse manure from the stables, to help their plants grow. It was my job to deliver it to them and, as a result, I developed an interest in the plants they grew there. I'm sure Judith has told you a lot about them, but they really have a wonderful collection of plants, many of which cannot be found in this country. Some need to be kept in heated greenhouses..."

Thomas paused, realising that his enthusiasm for the Gardens had led him away from the main question.

"Anyway," he continued, "I saw Judith in the Gardens on a number of occasions, either walking around with her young charges, or sometimes on her own, sketching the plants in a large notebook. I had seen her a few times at the livery stable, usually with the Hart family, but had never had the chance to speak to her. One day, I plucked up courage enough to approach her as she was sketching and complimented her on her drawing – she really is quite skilful in that respect, you know – one thing led to another and we have spent a lot of time since in each other's company."

It was obvious to both Isaac and Elizabeth how matters were developing and it would now be up to Isaac to have a private conversation with Thomas, so they brought the inquisition to an end until after they had eaten.

After the meal, Isaac took Thomas to the *Prince of Wales* and, after he had deposited his baggage in his room, Thomas joined Isaac for a drink. Isaac was quick to come to the point.

"Well, Thomas, it's obvious that Judith thinks a lot of you and I must say that I am impressed by you so far. Perhaps you have something to ask of me?"

Thomas was slightly taken aback by this direct approach. He had been wondering about how he would bring any conversation around to the matter that weighed most heavily on him, but had not imagined that Isaac would make it so easy.

"Well, sir, I hope that you have formed a good opinion of me, because it is my wish and intention to marry Judith. I could not do so, however, without your blessing. I would like to ask for your permission to marry your daughter."

After a suitable pause, Isaac gave his reply. "I see. Of course you must realise that it is not only my opinion of you that counts." Isaac was enjoying teasing the young man. "My wife can have a great influence on Judith, so she too must be convinced."

Thomas started to remonstrate. "But…"

"Oh, don't worry," said Isaac, cutting him short, "I have already spoken to her and she likes you." Another pause ensued, before Isaac finally put Thomas out of his misery. "As do I. You have both our blessings. I feel sure that you have already discussed this with Judith. Do you have any idea when the wedding will take place?"

A rather relieved Thomas took a long swig from his tankard, before answering.

"Well, we have to consider Judith's work with the Hart family. The daughter she was first with is no longer her responsibility, but she is now governess to their other sons, who are five and seven. It is likely that she will finish with them in the next two years, when their schooling is more formal. Then I would want to take on responsibility for her. We would expect to marry in late 1770."

"That sounds excellent. Tomorrow you can tell my daughter that her parents fully approve of your plans. I hope you will join us for all our Christmas celebrations and we will go to All Saints Church on Christmas Day, followed by our traditional dinner at Judith's grandparents' inn, the *Eight Bells*. I will warn them to expect an extra guest. Now let us charge our tankards once more and drink to your future happiness."

*   *   *   *   *

In the June of 1769, Isaac was at home, enjoying a brief break from the loft, while he enjoyed his lunch of bread and cheese. There was a knock at the door and, when Isaac opened it, he saw a liveried servant with a letter. He recognised the livery as belonging to the Turner family.

"Mr Isaac Forster?"

Isaac nodded and the man handed him the letter, saying briefly, "From Sir John Turner." With that he departed, leaving Isaac rather bemused. Why should Sir John be writing to him? He had done little business with the Turners and had never been a supporter of Sir John in his parliamentary campaigns.

He went back inside and broke the seal on the letter. Its contents did little to answer the question as to what Sir John wanted.

"Dear Mr Forster.

Sir John Turner, Mayor of King's Lynn, would like you to attend them at the Duke's Head, this evening at seven o'clock.

With Regards, Sir John Turner, Bart."

No matter how often Isaac read this short letter, he knew only two things. This was tantamount to a summons, which he could not ignore, and going to this meeting would be the only way to find out what this was all about.

Consequently, with the clock of St Margaret's standing at shortly after six thirty, Isaac set off to walk along Briggate to the *Duke's Head.* He had changed into his best suit and wore a freshly powdered wig. The walk was not long and he arrived at his destination with ten minutes to spare. After entering the tavern part of the building, he went up a flight of stairs to where he knew the Turners' private rooms to be and knocked at the door at the top of the stairs. It was opened by another liveried servant, who briefly scrutinised the letter that Isaac had received and then led him down a short corridor and into a parlour. He invited Isaac to sit at a chaise longue.

"Sir John and his brother will join you shortly, sir," he said, before leaving Isaac sitting there on his own.

Isaac settled back on the chaise longue and looked around the room. As befitted a family as wealthy as the Turners, it was furnished in an opulent style. This in itself did not come as a surprise to Isaac, as he had seen similar furniture and ornaments in Stephen Allen's house, but he could see that this was perhaps a step up from that. The chaise longue on which he was sitting was matched by two large chairs in a similar style, covered with identical brocade upholstery. The three pieces of furniture formed a group opposite a large fireplace. On the walls at either ends of the room were two large portrait paintings. Isaac immediately recognised them as the two gentlemen he was due to meet, Sir John and Charles Turner. In both of the portraits the subject was depicted in the robes of the Mayor of King's Lynn. The portraits obviously dated from the years in which each had served previously; Sir John in 1748 and Charles in 1759. Along the wall opposite the door by which he had entered, Isaac saw that there were more portraits. Isaac guessed, correctly, that these were more of the Turner family, although he had never seen any of them, when they were alive. One of the early portraits depicted a previous Sir John Turner, who had had commissioned Henry Bell to build several buildings in the town, including the *Duke's Head* itself.

As he continued to take stock of his surroundings, the door opened and Sir John and Charles Turner entered, followed by a manservant, who waited by the door. Isaac stood up and found that the hand of Sir John was extended towards him. He shook it, followed by that of Charles Turner.

"Sit down please, Mr Forster," said Sir John, "Would you like some wine?"

"Thank you, sir. That would be most kind."

As Isaac resumed his place, Sir John raised a hand in the direction of the manservant, who left the room. The two other men sat in the two chairs, facing Isaac. Almost before they were settled, the servant returned with a tray and on it a carafe of red wine and three glasses. He served each of them with a glassful of wine, before once again retiring from the room. Sir John began to speak.

"Mr Forster, or may we call you Isaac?" Isaac replied in the affirmative. The Mayor continued.

"Isaac, as you will know, I am currently Mayor of our fine town and my brother here was the Mayor last year. You will also have seen that, when the Mayor is on official business and goes in procession with the Aldermen and Common Councillors of the Corporation, he is preceded by a small group of officials, including four Sergeants at Mace and a Swordbearer."

"Yes, Mr Mayor," replied Isaac, "I have often seen this over the years."

"Well, unfortunately last year the Swordbearer, Giles Beeton died. We did not find a replacement in time for the normal appointments to office in August and the post has been filled, on a temporary basis, by the town gaoler, William Street, but this cannot be a long term solution."

Now Charles Turner intervened, "You see, Isaac, we like to have as our Swordbearer a citizen who has given good service to the town over a number of years. In your time, you have served as a constable for two years and as a headborough for nine. You have shown yourself willing to help the community when called upon to do so. The matter has been discussed among the Aldermen and we would like to offer you the position of Swordbearer."

Although Isaac had seen where the conversation was leading, he was still taken aback by the last statement and did not reply immediately. This led to Sir John speaking again.

"Well, sir. Will you agree? The post does come with a salary from the town, you know."

Isaac had recovered his composure and gave his reply. "Sir John, I am greatly honoured by this offer, which I gladly accept. I thank you both for considering me worthy of this position."

This short speech relieved the tension and both the Turners sat back in their chairs, smiling and exchanging looks of satisfaction.

"Well done, Isaac," said Sir John, "Now let us finish this fine wine and perhaps some more. Don't worry, we'll send you home in a carriage!"

Which, several hours and several carafes later, is precisely what happened.

Chapter Eighteen: Wharfinger

Although Isaac was not due to take up his duties as Swordbearer until August, there were still various matters to be settled before then. He had to be fitted out with the official ceremonial costume, consisting of a black suit, black stockings, black shoes and a white shirt, with a lace ruff collar. Over this he wore a long cloak, with gold braid trimmings. His crowning glory was a bicorn hat, again adorned with gold braid. The Corporation had a number of these ceremonial uniforms and one was found that was near his size. This was altered by a tailor to fit him precisely. Only the shoes were made especially for him, as it was recognised that, with having to walk a lot in procession, he needed to be comfortable.

He was instructed in his duties by one of the Sergeants at Mace, Robert Rollett. Isaac was familiar with Rollett, as the latter had been one of the advocates in the Guildhall Court, during Isaac's time as a headborough. He had held the position of Sergeant at Mace for several years, so was an ideal person to explain to Isaac the workings of the Mayor's procession.

At the front of the procession, there was the Town Beadle, with his staff of office, and the Town Crier. Behind them came the four Sergeants at Mace, walking two abreast. Next in line, on his own, would be Isaac, as the Swordbearer, and then the Mayor, his deputy, and all the other Aldermen and Common Councillors following behind in their robes.

Robert Rollett also took Isaac to visit the three churches that the Mayor was likely to visit officially; St Margaret's, St Nicholas Chapel and All Saints. In each he pointed out the sword rest and the pews that were reserved for the ceremonial officers. Finally, he took Isaac into the Treasury in the Guildhall, where all the town's precious objects were kept. Isaac had seen a few of these at a distance, but never before close to. Naturally he was most interested in the ceremonial sword. It was a large two-handed sword, of mediaeval pattern, encased in a red velvet-covered sheath, adorned with gold-coloured fittings, embossed with various symbols of the town and the nation. In the processions, it was carried unsheathed and with the point upwards. Isaac could now feel its weight and was a bit surprised at how light it felt. Swords of this pattern, when used in battle, would need to be wielded with both hands, the hilt being long enough to accommodate this, but when carried upright, as it would be in procession, Isaac could manage it easily with just one hand. Now he could also study the crosspiece above the hilt, on which there were two Latin inscriptions. On one side was written

Ensis hic Donum fuit Regis Johannis, a suo ipsius Latere datum.
(King John took this sword from his own side, and gave it [to this town].)

On the other side of the hilt was the inscription

Vivat Rex Henricus Octavus, Anno Regni sui xx
(Long live HenryVIII, in the twentieth year of his reign)

Although Isaac had had a rudimentary grounding in Latin when younger, he had to rely on Robert Rollett to provide him with the translations, but the learned gentleman did say that the first one was almost certainly not true. It was thought that both inscriptions had been made on the sword at the same time, during the reign of Henry VIII. However, the town's records did show that a sword was carried in procession as early as the reign of Henry III, in the late thirteenth century.

Isaac continued to look around the Treasury. As well as the sword and the four maces, there were a number of silver salvers and cups, as well as other plate. But one object really drew his attention. It was a large cup, made of silver gilt, elaborately decorated. The lid of the cup was surmounted by an ornamental finial and its sides had enamelled panels, with scenes depicting country pursuits, such as hunting with hawks.

"What is that?" asked Isaac, in awe.

"Ah yes," replied his mentor, "that is called King John's Cup. Local legend has it that it was also given to the town by King John, but I'm told by some who should know that the costumes in the enamelled panels are more like those of the fourteenth century, whilst some of the decoration is of a style later still. However, we do not discourage these legends; they give our citizens a sense of belonging to a town with a history stretching back over centuries."

Now that Isaac was fully informed of his duties and equipped with his ceremonial dress, all that remained was for the Mayor and Corporation to confirm him in the post. This occurred at a Congregation in the Guildhall, on the twenty-ninth of August, which was the Feast of the Decollation of John the Baptist, when all the town's officers were elected and sworn in.

Isaac felt a great sense of pride each and every time that he was called upon to act as Swordbearer. The Mayor would attend church each Sunday, as well as other major church festivals. Then there were also the other official occasions, such as the opening of the annual Mart, when the Mayor's procession to the Tuesday Market Place would usually be accompanied by drummers and other musicians. Any official announcements made by the Mayor, concerning matters of national importance, would also require the full turnout of officials. King's Lynn enjoyed its ceremonial and Isaac was proud of having been chosen to be a part of it. He now felt that, having started out as an orphan dependent on the charity of the parish, he had made his mark in the community. It was a position that he would enjoy for the rest of his life.

*   *   *   *   *

Having returned from one such procession, towards the end of the year, Isaac was taken aside by the Mayor. By this time the role had been taken on by another major merchant in the town, Samuel Browne (no relation to Isaac's assistant in the sail loft). Samuel Browne had a large house on Lath Street, which Isaac had often passed, particularly when he made his way from the cottage in Priory Lane to the Elstobb sail loft.

"Isaac, a word with you, please. I believe you know Griffith Jenkins."

"Yes, Mr Mayor. His son was an apprentice of mine."

"Well, since he retired from the sea, he has worked for the town as the Haven master, or wharfinger. You are familiar with the post?"

Isaac nodded. The wharfinger was responsible for collecting the tolls due to the town from ships that used the port.

The Mayor continued, "I'm afraid ill health is forcing him to resign and we need a replacement we can trust to maintain this valuable source of income to the town. Will you agree to take on the position. You will be allowed to keep five shillings of every pound that you collect as your salary."

Isaac thought for a moment, but not too long, as he quickly realised that this could prove a valuable source of income.

"Mr Mayor, I agree to accept the position." The two men shook hands. At the next congregation of the Corporation, on the twenty-ninth of January, Isaac was confirmed in the post and added the position of wharfinger to his civic duties.

Ships using the port of King's Lynn faced two possible demands for payment. The first came from the revenue men, who collected the national taxes. They were based in the Custom House, by the Purfleet. They would inspect the cargo of every ship, usually after it had been landed and taken into a warehouse, and from their calculations would levy the tax. Then there would be the town's wharfinger, who would exact payment for the passage of goods through the port, on behalf of the town. Isaac worked from a small brick building situated at the south end of the waterfront, close to the old Elstobb sail loft. There he had a desk, a chair, and a stove, fuelled with coal supplied by the town, who also supplied his stationery.

Each day, Isaac would spend several hours on the waterfront, making collections. Most goods owned by freemen of the town could be freely moved through the port, without any toll, so Isaac could concentrate on those ships and goods owned by those not from King's Lynn. He maintained a good relationship with the Custom House, as they would supply him with details of cargos. Then he would visit the ships' masters to collect the money.

This was not always easy. Many masters were unwilling to pay, especially those who did not understand why they had to pay twice for the same goods. Some tried bribes and even threats, but Isaac was persistent. His experiences as constable and headborough stood him in good stead when it came to negotiating. He also had the incentive that the more he collected, the more he would receive in commission. Isaac's ultimate weapon was the River Ouse. It was difficult to navigate through the various shallows and sandbanks, that shifted position on an almost seasonal basis. No master would risk his ship by attempting to regain the open sea without the help of a local pilot and no pilot would risk his licence by guiding a ship out of the port until Isaac had agreed that the proper tolls had been paid and given the master a receipt. For all their bluster, eventually everyone knew that they had to pay the town its due, or remain stranded in the port.

On the first Monday of each month, Isaac would meet the town's Chamberlain, John Sanderson, at the Guildhall, to settle the accounts. Isaac would supply the Chamberlain with a full account of every toll he had collected. Sanderson was happy for Isaac to deduct his commission before handing over the money and was pleased with the amounts that Isaac was collecting. As Isaac had expected, the commission, in addition to the thirteen pounds ten shillings he received annually as Swordbearer, was proving to be a welcome addition to his income. Of course, it did mean that he was away from the loft a great deal, but he had well-trained and trustworthy sail-makers in Samuel Browne and Henry Crow, whilst Henry Mickleson and William were nearly time-served and did not need close supervision. In any case, Isaac's time at the river-side was not all taken up with gathering tolls and he could talk to ships' masters and owners, which helped to drum up more work for the loft. As an added bonus, Isaac enjoyed his time in the fresh air. Taking all things into consideration, Isaac felt that this new job was a welcome addition to his life.

Chapter Nineteen: The Future

11ᵗʰ May 1770. It was a fine sunny morning. Shortly after eight o'clock, Isaac was already at his desk. Working at their benches were Henry Crow, Samuel Browne and Henry Mickleson. There was no sign, however, of William. Then the sound of footsteps coming up the stairs was heard and William entered the loft, a broad smile on his face. He exchanged cheerful greetings with his fellow sail-makers, before crossing towards Isaac's desk. Isaac stood up and moved around the desk, extending his right hand towards his son. As they met, Isaac, in a slightly uncharacteristic display of affection, pulled his son towards him and hugged him. Then he motioned William towards a chair and resumed his own behind the desk.

The importance of the occasion could be judged by the fact that William was in his best clothes, as was Isaac. Father and son looked at each other for a while, before Isaac spoke.

"My son, I'm proud of you. You've served your time and are now a fully qualified sail-maker. Before we go and complete matters at the Guildhall, let us drink to that."

He turned and, in what had been a tradition for Isaac with every one of his apprentices, took a stoppered bottle and two tankards from the shelf behind him. Not for him the small beer that his own master had served him, but some of Thomas Bonner's ale from the *Eight Bells*. However, mindful of where they would soon be, he only filled the tankards about two-thirds full. He handed one to William and raised his own tankard in salute.

"Here's to your health and to a job well done."

The toast was echoed by the others in the loft, although they would have to wait until later to make it with real liquor. After, drinking the ale, Isaac stood up and placed his hat on his head.

"Now we must be at the Guildhall, before the congregation starts at nine o'clock. Have you learnt the oath?" Isaac had managed to obtain a copy of the oath, so that William could be better prepared than he had been.

"Yes, father," replied the young man, also rising from his chair, "I am ready."

At that, the two men left the loft and descended to street level. The walk to the Guildhall was quite short. After walking down the narrow lane between Hampton Court on the right and the old Hanseatic Warehouses on the left, it was a simple matter to turn left and walk past St Margaret's Church and across the Saturday Market Place.

Once inside, they climbed the stairs to that same corridor that Isaac had first entered thirty-four years before. They sat together on the same bench and waited for the day's proceedings to begin. They were joined there by three other men; James Sacker, a peruke-maker and barber, Thomas Harrison and Robert Carrow, both innkeepers. They were all well known to Isaac and greeted him warmly. At this point, the door of the Robing Room opened at the end of the corridor and the members of the Council filed past into the main council chamber. All those waiting stood in respect until the procession had entered the Council Chamber.

After a few minutes, the Town Clerk, Scarlet Browne, appeared to speak to them.

"Gentlemen, there's not too much business today, so you shouldn't have to wait too long."

Isaac was glad to hear this, as he knew that freedom oaths came at the end of the meeting and on occasions he had spent most of the day in this corridor. The Town Clerk continued, "Mr Sacker, the matter of your loan will be dealt with after the Treasury is formally opened. I see you have your three sureties here, so you can complete matters today. And then, Isaac, we can deal with young William here."

With that, Scarlet Browne re-entered the chamber. William was a little mystified by one thing."

"Father, the Town Clerk mentioned three sureties, but I only see two people with Mr Sacker. How is this?"

Isaac chuckled. "You see, William, I'm not just here for you today. I am James's third surety. Many years ago, I started my business with just such a loan and three of my friends stood surety for me. I am only too happy to give James here a helping hand, as he starts out on his own. I shall be going in with him at the appropriate time."

And so it was that Isaac went into the chamber in support of his friend, who was obtaining twenty pounds from the same fund that Isaac had received to start his own business. It seemed to Isaac at this point that, although his main purpose for being there was to look to the future, there were many reminders of the past as well.

At last it was William's turn. He walked proudly into the chamber at his father's side. The ceremony was identical to the one experienced by Isaac in 1736. If anything, the members of the Council were more relaxed than usual, as they knew Isaac so well as the Swordbearer. Isaac had, of course, now witnessed quite a few freedom ceremonies, as each of his apprentices had been presented as freemen of the town. The latest had been only a few months previously, when Henry Mickleson finished his term. Naturally, he felt a special pride in the recipient being his own son. At the same time, he also knew that this would probably be the last time he would be here in this capacity, as he had no need, nor intention, to take on further apprentices.

As they left the Guildhall and made their way back towards Hampton Court, the church clock was striking twelve. Isaac turned to his son.

"Well, William, now you're one of the paid workers. Better get back home and change into your working clothes. There's plenty to be done this afternoon."

Isaac had to smile at his son's crestfallen look. "What did he expect?" he thought.

"Don't worry, William, there'll be time to celebrate later. The whole loft and a few other friends have been invited to join us for drinks at the *Prince of Wales,* later." With that, Isaac hurried off in the direction of the river, to catch up with his duties as wharfinger.

As promised, there was a celebration that evening, where William could begin to officially enjoy the pleasures of adulthood. The ale and beer flowed freely, at Isaac's expense. Isaac mused that he would need to be particularly efficient at collecting tolls in the next few weeks, in order to pay this account.

At the end of the evening, Isaac was sitting at a table across from his son, obviously very happy, but now showing the effects of the drink and finding difficulty in staying awake. Isaac was in a reflective mood. In front of him he saw his only son, who would carry his name forward. He himself had managed to build a life from a poor start to one where he could give his family a relatively comfortable existence. For that he had to thank all those who had helped him along the way; his master, William Elstobb, Margaret and their two sons, William and poor Nicholas, Stephen Allen and his son, friends who had stood surety for his loan, as he had done today for James Sacker, and so the list went on. His daughters were all settled into good jobs and one of them, Judith, would be married later that year. He wondered what lay ahead for William. He hoped he would build on the start that he had been given. Above all, Isaac thought that this day he had been as proud and happy as on any day since the 20th May 1736.

FACT OR FICTION?

This story has been based on the lives of real people and events, but, as might be expected, there simply isn't enough information available for it to be completely factual. For the most part, names and occupations mentioned are those of actual people, using as much information as I can find about them from various sources. Here I will try to explain what has been invented and what is fact. If anyone has a particular interest in any of the people mentioned, please feel free to contact me and I will direct them to my sources.

Chapter One: A New Beginning

We know from the Hall Books that Isaac Forster completed his apprenticeship under William Elstobb and was made a Freeman of the Borough on 20th May 1736. We also have a clear idea, from descriptions in H J Hillen's book (see Bibliography) and from the Oath Rolls and other documents in the Borough Archives, of the oath that he would have taken and the type of ceremony he would have undergone.

What are less sure are the facts about Isaac's early life. I can find no record in parish registers of his baptism, or his family. I have assumed, therefore, that he was an orphan and was apprenticed to William with the help of the parish, as was often the case at that time.

I also have no evidence as to where the sail loft was situated, nor where the Elstobbs lived, apart from the fact that both they and, later, the Forsters had a close association with the parish of South Lynn and All Saints Church. Having walked over the area during my visits to King's Lynn, I have placed these venues in what I would consider to be logical positions.

The names of the streets are those given on maps from the period or soon after. For example, what is now Nelson Street was then Lath (or sometimes Lathe) Street, whilst the current High Street was known as Briggate, prior to the nineteenth century.

Chapter Two: High Days and Holidays

Up until 1752, England used the Julian Calendar and the days and dates used in this book correspond to that, until the story reaches 1752. Easter in England was indeed late that year and the Prince of Wales did marry a few days later. Undoubtedly, this Royal occasion would have been celebrated in the town.

The description of the Mayor's procession is based on the sketch by the Rev. Edward Edwards, as illustrated in David Higgins' book. Current-day processions follow a similar pattern. All the churches have a sword rest in them.

There is very little to be found about the Bonner family and they do not appear in the parish records, so may have come from elsewhere, but a later Bonner in King's Lynn was in the brewery trade, so I have used this as a starting point for my depiction of the family.

The description of the entertainment to be found in the Tuesday Market Place is based on similar events described by Hillen.

There was a public house called the *Eight Bells*, situated in about this area. The information about ale and beer is taken from Kirstin Olsen's book.

Chapter Three: Courtship and Departure

Most of this chapter is pure invention. William junior did, apparently, take longer than usual over his apprenticeship and did eventually become a surveyor, rather than a sail-maker, so this fits the facts. And, of course, Isaac did court Elizabeth over quite a period of time.

The reference to the poems of Isaac Thompson is borne out by the fact that the list of subscribers printed in the book, published in 1731, includes a number of people from King's Lynn, including William and Margaret Elstobb. David Samuel, a local printer, subscribed for six copies, so he is almost certainly the person to have acted as the agent. There is a subscription for a Mrs Mary Elstobb, but I have not been able to find out who this is.

Chapter 4: The path of true love...

Again, mostly fiction. The Christmas feast is based on one described in Kirstin Olson's book. The Mart still continues to this day, although those familiar with it will know that it now starts on February 14th, St Valentine's Day. This discrepancy is probably due to the eleven day change in the calendar, when, in 1752, England changed from the Julian calendar to the Gregorian.

Chapter Five: Changes

In order to fit in with the time-scale of Isaac getting married in 1739 and later becoming his own master, together with other evidence of the likely pattern of events, this narrative fits the known facts.

Chapter Six: O Happy Day!

This was indeed the date and place of Isaac's wedding, but we have to imagine what it would have been like. For this, Kirstin Olsen's book has been invaluable in throwing a light on contemporary wedding customs, whilst the order of service would have followed that in the Book of Common Prayer, for which I have gone back to the 1681 edition, in use at that time.

The cottage, to which Isaac and Elizabeth move, is an invention. The location is a possible one and the description of the cottage is based on similar cottages in True's Yard.

Chapter Seven: Mixed Fortunes

The time of the birth of Isaac's first child can be estimated from the baptismal records of St Margaret's Church.

The storm of 1741 and the damage it caused are described in Hillen and elsewhere. The Hall Books record the fact that a letter was later sent to Sir Robert Walpole, asking for his help.

Through the records on the LDS web site, it has been ascertained that Nicholas had a Quaker wedding. The format of this wedding is described in various places on the internet and I have also attended the wedding of some Quaker friends, which followed a broadly similar pattern. Norfolk Record Office has deeds which show that Nicholas was involved in land deals on behalf of the Quakers, mainly for burial sites. The records of his wedding state that it took place in "Stoak" (sic), but I have moved it to King's Lynn itself for the purposes of this story. It is not clear exactly where the meeting house was at this time; there was certainly one in New Conduit Street at a later date and the venue given here is one that is mentioned as being one of their meeting places.

Chapter Eight: Changes

This chapter is strongly based on actual records. The additions to the family can be deduced once more from baptismal records.

In 1745, Isaac did take out a loan from the corporation, with the three sureties mentioned. This is recorded in the Hall Books. It was also at about this time that he is recorded as living at Hampton Court, which was in the ownership of Stephen Allen, a wine merchant. I have, therefore, based his new sail loft in warehouses that adjoin Hampton Court, between it and the river. Although the evidence is circumstantial, it would seem that it was at about this time that Isaac became his own master.

Chapter Nine: Alarms, Tragedy and Democracy.

The effect of the campaign of the Young Pretender on the town is well-documented in the various histories cited in the Bibliography and these are the source of this section of the chapter.

That Isaac's first born died in infancy is highly likely, as he gives the same name to a later child. There is a burial record for a Susanna Forster at this time, but with no details of age or parentage. The symptoms ascribed to the child's fatal illness are consistent with influenza, turning eventually to pneumonia.

Daniel Locust was a former apprentice of William Elstobb, but I have used the history of Anson's expedition to add some "colour" to his character. There is much more information to be found on the internet about this expedition and it has itself been used as the inspiration for other novels.

Again, the histories are the source of information on the election campaign of 1747. An eye-witness report from an anonymous letter writer is quoted in length in William Richards' book (vol. II, pp948-52) and, from this account, it is possible to identify many of the leading figures in the campaign. There is even mention of Nicholas and the state he and John Harvey were in after the result, as well as Harvey's subsequent death and funeral. The Poll Books show which voters voted at about the same time, and also who "plumped" for Folkes. It is from these that I have drawn the names of the group that made their way to the hustings with Isaac. The description of the voting booth and hustings is based on one found in the copy of the Poll for the 1822 election.

Chapter Ten: Additions and Responsibilities

The taking on of his first apprentice, his service as a constable for two years and the birth of his children are all facts recorded in the various records cited in the Bibliography. My fictional account attempts to breathe some life into these cold facts.

Chapter Eleven: A Time of Death

Nicholas Elstobb died on the date stated and was given a Quaker funeral. This much can be gleaned from the records that are left. His illness was briefly mentioned in the eye-witness account in William Richards' book (see above; Chapter Nine).

I have drawn on descriptions of Quaker funerals for that of Nicholas. It is also possible to see, from the Hall Books, that Mary carried on the sail-making business until at least the time that the two apprentices finished their term. It is not unreasonable to think that she would have had help from other sympathetic sail-makers, including Isaac.

The crimes and trial of Charles Holditch are fairly well documented in various sources and I have drawn mainly from Hillen for this description. Since it occurred at a time around the end of Isaac's service as a constable, I have given him a part to play in the story.

Other events in this chapter – the apprenticeship of Samuel Browne and the identity of his sponsor, the death of the Prince of Wales, Stephen Allen's death and the change to the Gregorian calendar all took place at this time and are recorded in various sources.

Chapter Twelve: Education and Service

Most of the facts, around which the events in this chapter are based, can be found in the Hall Books for the time. The positions that William Elstobb the younger held in the town, as chamberlain, surveyor and schoolmaster, are recorded there.

This was also the start of a nine year period when Isaac served as headborough for the Stonegate ward. The names of his companions as constable and headborough have also been found in the Hall Books and the Leet Rolls, whilst their occupations have, for the main part, been found in the Poll Books for 1747 and 1768.

The Perambulation, or "beating the bounds", was part of the life of every parish in the country and was the way that the young were taught the limits of their home parish. The description here is based on descriptions given by Hillen of typical Permabulations, particularly in South Lynn. The parish accounts include an item of money paid to "*the boys for being wipt at ye dewels*". St Margaret's accounts also give a list of the persons paid for supplying the food and drink.

The circumstances of the death of George II are also well documented in various sources.

Chapter Thirteen: A Move to Pastures New

At some point in her life, Sarah moved to the London area and eventually got married. This I know from later evidence found in her brother's will. With this slimmest of factual evidence, I have invented a possible reason for her move in the first place.

Chapter Fourteen: New Friendships

Thomas Sharpe served three years as constable, alongside Isaac and John Hart as headborough. The families obviously became better acquainted, since young William is destined to eventually marry Ann Sharpe. Around this time, John Hart is mentioned in two different capacities. There are deeds in Norfolk Record Office that give his trade as a rope-maker, whilst other sources, such as the Poll Book for 1768, say he is a merchant. Later, he appears in the lists of councillors for the town. These could have been two different John Harts, or perhaps the same person, who has fulfilled his ambitions. I have chosen to use the latter as the basis for his story.

The story of the whale is well-documented in the histories and also in the Norfolk and Norwich Remembrancer, which covers major events in the county from 1701 to 1821. No doubt such an event would have drawn great crowds from the surrounding areas to see this wonder of the deep.

Chapter Fifteen: A Year of Change

1763 was an important year for Isaac. Most of the events described in this chapter are based on what is recorded in the Hall Books and other sources. Once again, I have had to find a story to explain Judith's move to Cambridge, as she will eventually marry there.

The tower at All Saints collapsed in 1763 and I have tried to imagine the effect this might have had on Isaac and Elizabeth. This was "their" church; they had married there and would eventually be laid to rest there.

Stephen Allen did die at this time and it seemed that his illness was indeed a long one. He missed a number of council congregations, being excused on the grounds of illness. He also wrote his final will in the February of 1763.

At about this time, judging by the time he finished and received his freedom, William started his apprenticeship. The information about sails on the ships of the time and how they were made has been derived from a number of online sources, but principally from Robert Kipping's book *"The Elements of Sailmaking"*. Although this was published nearly a century later, very little would have changed, apart from some of the materials used.

Chapter Sixteen: The End of an Era

See the comments for the previous chapter on the sources for information on sail-making.

Unlike her sisters, Susanna appears not to have left King's Lynn, nor married. I have, therefore, "found" her a position locally.

William Elstobb lived to a ripe old age and this is confirmed by the record of his burial. However, there is some evidence that he was in straitened circumstances towards the end of his life. At Christmas 1762, he is listed in the Hall Books as having received £2 – 2s – 0d from a charitable fund, the maximum amount awarded.

When he died in 1766, he received a Quaker burial, like his son and wife before him. We can assume that this would have been well attended, as he had touched so many other lives in the town.

Chapter Seventeen: Swordbearer

I know from the 1768 poll book, that John Jenkins, Edward Barratt and Thomas Tilson were then based in London, returning to the town to vote in the election. I have also found records that show that John Jenkins took on an apprentice of his own in later years. This narrative explains that move.

The description of the 1768 General Election campaign is based on accounts in Hillen and also various sources on the history behind the John Wilkes case.

Giles Beeton did die at around this time and his funeral was two days after the election. He was married to Sarah Burch, Thomas's sister. He is mentioned several times in the Leet Rolls as an affeeror and it would seem that this position was not given to just anybody, so I have set his status as a merchant, although not in the top rank. He was the Swordbearer before Isaac, but, although he died in March 1768, he was not replaced until August 1769. One possible explanation of this could lie in the fact that the Corporation were evenly divided into pro and anti Turner camps, according to the Poll Books. Perhaps it took them some time to agree on a suitable candidate. After all, Isaac was not a Turner supporter. The Chamberlain's Accounts show that William Street, the gaoler, was paid a year's salary as a stand-in, whilst Sarah Beeton, widow of Giles, was paid a half year's salary.

Judith is due to marry Thomas Randale in November 1770, in Cambridge, so I have used my imagination (again!) to make a plausible story.

Sir John Turner was the Mayor in 1769, and his brother, Charles, had been the Mayor before him. It seems likely that they would have made the offer of Swordbearer to Isaac. Where better than in their own rooms at the *Duke's Head*?

Chapter Eighteen: Wharfinger

As mentioned above (Chapter Two), we have a sketch of the Mayor's procession, plus photographs of the modern day officials. I have based my description of the dress on these sources, taking into account the style of clothing at that time. The other items in the Treasury, such as King John's Cup and King John's Sword, are on view in the Guildhall in King's Lynn. The inscriptions on the sword, and their translations, plus details of the cup, are to be found in William Taylor's book, *The Antiquities of King's Lynn, Norfolk.*

Isaac did take over as wharfinger from Griffith Jenkins and was to stay in the post until his death. From the figures given in the Chamberlain's account books of the tolls collected, from which Isaac had already taken his "cut", it would seem that this job was worth £60 to £70 a year, which, in simple terms of inflation, is the equivalent of around £7,000 today. It would be worth considerably more in terms of Isaac's status in the community. For example, the Mayor's salary at that time was £100 a year.

The description of the problems he may have encountered in collecting money has been based on ones described in the Custom House, with respect to the Revenue men.

Chapter Nineteen: The Future

Here the story comes full circle. William gains his freedom of the town in the same manner as did Isaac in Chapter One. The Hall Books show that, on the same day as William is sworn as a freeman at the Guildhall, James Sacker takes out a loan and Isaac is one of his sureties. Another nice symmetry with earlier events, but it did actually happen that way.

This is the end of Isaac's story. He was to live another four years. Judith did get married in November 1770, but there is no marriage for Sarah until much later and none that I can find for Susannah. As for William's future...? Perhaps you'll have to wait for a sequel.

BIBLIOGRAPHY

Edited by Antonia Fraser *The Lives of the Kings and Queens of England (1975, paperback edition 1997)*

David Higgins   *The Antiquities of King's Lynn (2001)*

Henry J Hillen   *History of the Borough of King's Lynn (in two volumes) (1907)* *

Robert Kipping   *The Elements of Sailmaking (1847)* *

B Mackerell   *The History & Antiquities of the flourishing corporation of King's Lynn (1738)* *

Norfolk Chronicle Mecum (1822)* *   *Norfolk and Norwich Remembrancerand Vade*

Kirstin Olsen   *Daily Life in 18th Century England (1999)* *

William Richards   *The History of Lynn (in two volumes) (1812)* *

Paul Richards   *King's Lynn (1990)*

William Taylor   *The Antiquities of King's Lynn, Norfolk (1844)* *

Isaac Thompson   *A Collection of Poems (1731)* *

A correct copy of the poll at an election for a burgess to serve in parliament for the borough of King's Lynn... June 27th, 1822 (1822) *

The Book of Common Prayer (1681) *

The Two Books of Homilies (originally published 16th century. Reprinted 1859) *

These items were all available via the internet, from Google Play or Kindle..

The other main resources used were:

Norfolk Record Office – Parish Registers, Wills, Maps and various other Deeds and Indentures.

King's Lynn Archives – Hall Books, Calendar of the Freemen of King's Lynn, Apprentice Records, Leet Rolls, Oath Rolls, Chamberlain's Accounts and many other documents, as well as access to research by local historians

Multiple internet sites (far too many to list) were consulted, starting with Google Search. Another major resource was the LDS web site *htpps://familysearch.org* which contains many records, including copies of Parish Records and access to Quaker records. The Genuki site *http://www.genuki.org.uk/* is another potent resource. In particular, copies of Poll Books for contested elections can be found there, showing exactly how everyone voted.

ACKNOWLEDGEMENTS

During the preparation of this novel, many of my family and friends have given me great encouragement, through reading various parts of the book and giving me their feedback and suggestions. I would like to thank them all – they know who they are.

ABOUT THE AUTHOR

Robert Merry – usually known as Bob – is now a semi-retired professional fencing coach, teaching the sport in schools and clubs. He served ten years in the RAF, mainly as an instructor on various aspects of radar, wireless and electronics. He then spent nearly twenty-five years as a vision engineer with Granada TV, before taking early retirement to spend more time coaching fencing.

Although this is his first attempt at a novel, he has had various other works published. These include articles for computer magazines and a broad range of material, covering general electronics and television, for a major correspondence school.

His interest in family history research dates back a long way and has been actively pursued since the 1970s.

If this book has helped any readers with their own research and they wish to find out more, direct from the author, he can be contacted on bobmerrybaf@aol.com.

Printed by Amazon Italia Logistica S.r.l.
Torrazza Piemonte (TO), Italy

11069603R00113